ORBIT 3

"This, the third edition of Mr. Knight's Orbit series, features original science fiction stories which have not appeared previously anywhere. The material has been chosen with an eye to both variety and originality. A novelette by John Jakes, 'Here Is Thy Sting,' manages to make death both rousing and quite amusing—a *tour de force* indeed. The lead story, 'Mother to the World,' by Richard Wilson, is a moving variation on the Last Man theme. The late Richard McKenna, author of 'The Sand Pebbles,' has a story, 'Bramble Bush,' which is good enough to indicate he could have been a top s-f writer had he lived to write more of the same. Perhaps the strongest story is Kate Wilhelm's 'The Planners' in which science fiction remains in its own metier, yet becomes disturbingly real.

"A must for discerning science fiction buffs, this is possibly the best of the Orbit series yet, a high rating indeed."

—*Publishers' Weekly*

ORBIT 3

Edited by
DAMON KNIGHT

A BERKLEY MEDALLION BOOK
published by
BERKLEY PUBLISHING CORPORATION

BERKLEY MEDALLION EDITION, SEPTEMBER, 1968

BERKLEY MEDALLION BOOKS are published by
Berkley Publishing Corporation
200 Madison Avenue
New York, N.Y. 10016

BERKLEY MEDALLION BOOKS ® TM 757,375

Printed in the United States of America

CONTENTS

Science fiction writers sometimes seem to be engaged in a witty but very leisurely debate, in which decades may pass between one comment and the next. Thus Mary Wollstonecraft Shelley's The Last Man *(1826) was followed in turn by M. P. Shiel's* The Purple Cloud *(1929), Alfred Bester's "Adam and No Eve" (1941), Fredric Brown's "Knock" (1948), and my own "Not With a Bang" (1950), among others.*

Each of these writers probably felt he had said the last word; I know I did. But again and again, when a theme like this appears to be exhausted, along comes another writer who picks it up and turns it by some magic into a fresh, new thing.

Richard Wilson's "Mother to the World" is not just a new variation on the Last Man theme; he has given it one new twist, which I will not mention, since he reveals it himself in the first three hundred words, but it's a rather unimportant technicality anyhow. What is important is not the variation but what Wilson has made of it—this deeply honest, memorable and moving story.

Mother To The World

by Richard Wilson

His name was Martin Rolfe. She called him Mr. Ralph.
She was Cecelia Beamer, called Siss.

He was a vigorous, intelligent, lean and wiry forty-two,
a shade under six feet tall. His hair, black, was thinning
but still covered all of his head; and all his teeth were his
own. His health was excellent. He'd never had a cavity or
an operation and he fervently hoped he never would.

She was a slender, strong young woman of twenty-
eight, five feet four. Her eyes, nose and mouth were regular and well-spaced but the combination fell short of
beauty. She wore her hair, which was dark blonde, not
quite brown, straight back and long in two pigtails which
she braided daily, after a ritualistic hundred brushings.
Her figure was better than average for her age and therefore good, but she did nothing to emphasize it. Her dispo-
sition was cheerful when she was with someone; when
alone her tendency was to work hard at the job at hand,
giving it her serious attention. Whatever she was doing
was the most important thing in the world to her just then
and she had a compulsion to do it absolutely right. She
was indefatigable but she liked, almost demanded, to be
praised for what she did well.

Her amusements were simple ones. She liked to talk to
people but most people quickly became bored with what

she had to say—she was inclined to be repetitive. Fortunately for her, she also liked to talk to animals, birds included.

She was a retarded person with the mentality of an eight-year-old.

Eight can be a delightful age. Rolfe remembered his son at eight—bright, inquiring, beginning to emerge from childhood but not so fast as to lose any of his innocent charm; a refreshing, uninhibited conversationalist with an original viewpoint on life. The boy had been a challenge to him and a constant delight. He held on to that memory, drawing sustenance from it, for her.

Young Rolfe was dead now, along with his mother and three billion other people.

Rolfe and Siss were the only ones left in all the world.

It was M.R. that had done it, he told her. Massive Retaliation; from the Other Side.

When American bombs rained down from long-range jets and rocket carriers, nobody'd known the Chinese had what they had. Nobody'd suspected it of that relatively backward country which the United States had believed it was softening up, in a brushfire war, for enforced diplomacy.

Rolfe hadn't been aware of any speculation that Peking's scientists were concentrating their research not on weapons but on biochemistry. Germ warfare, sure. There'd been propaganda from both sides about that, but nothing had been hinted about a biological agent, as it must have been, that could break down human cells and release the water.

"M.R.," he told her. "Better than nerve gas or the neutron bomb." Like those, it left the buildings and equipment intact. Unlike them, it didn't leave any messy corpses—only the bones, which crumbled and blew away.

Except the bone dust trapped inside the pathetic mounds of clothing that lay everywhere in the city.

"Are they coming over now that they beat us?"

"I'm sure they intended to. But there can't be any of them left. They outsmarted themselves, I guess. The wind must have blown it right back at them. I don't really know what happened, Siss. All I know is that everybody's gone now, except you and me."

"But the animals—"

Rolfe had found it best in trying to explain something to Siss to keep it simple, especially when he didn't understand it himself. Just as he had learned long ago that if he didn't know how to pronounce a word he should say it loud and confidently.

So all he told Siss was that the bad people had got hold of a terrible weapon called M.R.—she'd heard of that—and used it on the good people and that nearly everybody had died. Not the animals, though, and damned if he knew why.

"Animals don't sin," Siss told him.

"That's as good an explanation as any I can think of," he said. She was silent for a while. Then she said: "Your name—initials—are M.R., aren't they?"

He'd never considered it before, but she was right. Martin Rolfe—Massive Retaliation. I hope she doesn't blame everything on me, he thought. But then she spoke again. "M.R. That's short for Mister. What I call you. Your name that I have for you. Mister Ralph."

"Tell me again how we were saved, Mr. Ralph."

She used the expression in an almost evangelical sense, making him uncomfortable. Rolfe was a practical man, a realist and freethinker.

"You know as well as I do, Siss," he said. "It's because Professor Cantwell was doing government research and because he was having a party. You certainly remember; Cantwell was your boss."

"I know that. But you tell it so good and I like to hear it."

"All right. Bill Cantwell was an old friend of mine from the army and when I came to New York I gave him a call at the University. It was the first time I'd talked to him in years; I had no idea he'd married again and had set up housekeeping in Manhattan."

"And had a working girl named Siss," she put in.

"The very same," he agreed. Siss never referred to herself as a maid, which was what she had been. "And so when I asked Bill if he could put me up, I thought it would be in his old bachelor apartment. He said sure, just like that, and I didn't find out till I got there, late in the evening, that he had a new wife and was having a house-party and had invited two couples from out of town to stay over."

"I gave my room to Mr. and Mrs. Glenn, from Columbus," Siss said.

"And the Torquemadas, of Seville, had the regular guest room." Whoever they were; he didn't remember names the way she did. "So that left two displaced persons, you and me."

"Except for the Nassers."

The Nassers, as she pronounced it, were the two self-contained rooms in the Cantwell basement. The NASAs, or the Nasas, was what Cantwell called them because the National Aeronautics and Space Administration had given him a contract to study the behavior of human beings in a closed system.

Actually the money had gone to Columbia University, where Cantwell was a professor of mechanical and aerospace engineering.

"A sealed-off environment," Rolfe said. "But because Columbia didn't have the space just at that time, and because the work was vital, NASA gave Cantwell permission to build the rooms in his own home. They were—still are—in his basement, and that's where you and I slept that fateful night when the world ended."

"I still don't understand."

"We were completely sealed off in there," Rolfe said. "We weren't breathing Earth air and we weren't connected in any way to the rest of the world. We might as well have been out in space or on the moon. So when it happened to everybody else—to Professor and Mrs. Cantwell, and to the Glenns and the Torquemadas and to the Nassers in Egypt and the Joneses in Jones Beach and all the people at Columbia, and in Washington and Moscow and Pretoria and London and Peoria and Medicine Hat and La Jolla and all those places all over—it didn't happen to us. That's because Professor Cantwell was a smart man and his closed systems worked."

"And we were saved."

"That's one way of looking at it."

"What's the other way?"

"We were doomed."

From his notebooks:

Siss asked why I'm so sure there's nobody but us left in the whole world. A fair question. Of course I'm not absolutely positively cross-my-heart-and-hope-to-die, swear-on-a-Bible convinced that there isn't a poor live slob hidden away in some remote corner. Other people besides Bill must have been working with closed systems; certainly any country with a space program would be, and maybe some of *their* nassers were inhabited, too. I hadn't heard that any astronauts or cosmonauts were in orbit that day but if they were, and got down safely, I guess they could be alive somewhere.

But I've listened to the rest of the world on some of the finest radio equipment ever put together and there hasn't been a peep out of it. I've listened and signaled and listened and signaled and listened. Nothing. Nil. Short wave, long wave, AM, FM, UHF, marine band, everywhere. Naught. Not a thing. Lots of automatic signals from unmanned satellites, of course, and the quasars are still being heard from, but nothing human.

I've sent out messages on every piece of equipment

connected to Con Ed's EE net. RCA, American Cable & Radio, the Bell System, Western Union, The Associated Press, UPI, Reuters' world news network, *The New York Times'* multifarious teletypes, even the Hilton Hotels' international reservations system. Nothing. By this time I'd become fairly expert at communications and I'd found the Pentagon network at AT&T. Silent. Ditto the hot line to the Kremlin. I read the monitor teletype and saw the final message from Washington to Moscow. Strictly routine. No hint that anything was amiss anywhere. Just as it must have been at the Army message center at Pearl Harbor on another Sunday morning a generation ago.

This is for posterity, these facts. My evidence is circumstantial. But to Siss I say: "There's nobody left but us. I know. You'll have to take my word for it that the rest of the world is as empty as New York."

Nobody here but us chickens, boss. Us poor flightless birds. One middle-aged rooster and one sad little hen, somewhat deficient in the upper story. What do you want us to do, boss? What's the next step in the great cosmic scheme? Tell us: where do we go from here?

But don't tell me; tell Siss. I don't expect an answer; she does. She's the one who went into the first church she found open that Sunday morning (some of them were locked, you know) and said all the prayers she knew, and asked for mercy for her relatives, and her friends, and her employers, and for me, and for all the dead people who had been alive only yesterday, and finally for herself; and then she asked why. She was in there for an hour and when she came out I don't think she'd had an answer.

Nobody here but us chickens, boss. What do you want us to do now, fricassee ourselves?

Late on the morning of doomsday they had taken a walk down Broadway, starting from Cantwell's house near the Columbia campus.

There were a number of laughs to be had from cars in comical positions, if anybody was in a laughing mood.

Some were standing obediently behind white lines at intersections, and obviously their drivers had been overtaken during a red light. With its driver gone, each such car had simply stood there, its engine dutifully using up all the gas in its tank and then coughing to a stop. Others had nosed gently into shop windows, or less gently into other cars or trucks. One truck, loaded with New Jersey eggs, had overturned and its cargo was dripping in a yellowy-white puddle. Rolfe, his nose twitching as if in anticipation of a warm day next week, made a mental note never to return to that particular spot.

Several times he found a car which had been run up upon from behind by another. It was as if, knowing they would never again be manufactured, they were trying copulation.

While Siss was in church Rolfe found a car that had not idled away all its gas and he made a dry run through the streets. He discovered that he could navigate pretty well around the stalled or wrecked cars, though occasionally he had to drive up on the sidewalk or make a three-block detour to get back to Broadway.

Then he and Siss, subdued after church, went downtown.

"Whose car is this, Mr. Ralph?" she asked him.

"My car, Siss. Would you like one, too?"

"I can't drive."

"I'll teach you. It may come in handy."

"I was the only one in church," she said. It hadn't got through to her yet, he thought; not completely.

"Who were you expecting?" he asked kindly.

"God, maybe."

She was gazing straight ahead, clutching her purse in her lap. She had the expression of a person who had been let down.

At 72nd Street a beer truck had demolished the box office of the Trans-Lux movie house and foamy liquid was still trickling out of it, across the sidewalk and along the gutter and into a sewer. Rolfe stopped the car and got out. An aluminum barrel had been punctured. The beer leaking from it was cool. He leaned over and let it run into his mouth for a while.

The Trans-Lux had been having a Fellini festival; the picture was *8½*. On impulse he went inside and came back to the car with the reels of film in a black tin box. He remembered the way the movie had opened, with all the cars stalled in traffic. Like Broadway, except that the Italian cars had people in them. He put the box in the rear of the car and said: "We'll go to the movies sometime." Siss looked at him blankly.

At Columbus Circle a Broadway bus had locked horns with a big van carrying furniture from North Carolina. At 50th Street a Mustang had nosed gently into the front of a steak house, as if someone had led it to a hitching post.

He made an illegal left turn at 42nd Street, noting what was playing at the Rialto: two naughty, daring, sexy, nudie pix, including a re-run of "My Bare Lady." He didn't stop for that one.

At the old Newsweek Building east of Broadway, an Impala had butted into the ground-floor liquor store. The plate glass lay smashed but the bottles in the window were intact. He made a mental note. Across the street, one flight up, was the Keppel Folding Boat Company, which had long intrigued him. Soon it might be useful to unfold one and sail off to a better place. He marked it in his mind.

Bookstores, 42nd Street style. Dirty books and magazines. Girly books. Deviant, flagellant, homosexual, Lesbian, sadistic books. Pornographic classics restored to the common man—*Memoirs of a Woman of Pleasure. The Kama Sutra,* quaint but lasciviously advertised. Books of nudes for the serious artist (no retoucher's airbrush here, men!).

Nudie pix in packets, wrapped in pliofilm, at a buck and a half the set. Large girls in successive states of undress. How big can a breast be before it disgusts? What is the optimum bosom size? A cup? D cup? It would depend on the number to be fed, wouldn't it? And how hungry they were? Or was that criterion passé?

He looked over at Siss, who wasn't looking at him or the bookstores or the dirty-movie houses but straight ahead. She had a nice figure. About a C.

But it was never the body alone; it was the mind that went with it and the voice with which it spoke.

"What are you thinking, Siss?" he asked.

"Nothing," she said. It was probably true. "What are *you* thinking?"

Riposte. How could he tell her?

He improvised. They were passing Bryant Park. "Pigeons in the park," he said. "I'm thinking of the pigeons. Hungrier than yesterday because nobody's buying peanuts for them, bringing slices of bread from home; there's no bread lady buying bagfuls for them at Horn & Hardart's day-old bakery shop."

"It's a sad time, isn't it, Mr. Ralph?"

"Yes, Siss; a sad time."

They got to First Avenue and the U.N. There wasn't anybody there, either.

Notes for a History of the World was what he wrote on page one of his notebook.

On page two he had alternate titles, some facetious:

The True History of the Martin Rolfe Family on the Planet Earth; or, *Two for Tomorrow.*

Recollections of a World Well Lost.

How the Population Crisis Was Solved.

What Next? or, if *You* Don't Do It, Marty, Who the Hell Will?

From his notebooks:

Thank God for movies. We'd be outen our minds by now if I hadn't taught myself to be a projectionist.

Radio City Music Hall apparently's only movie on Con Ed's EE list. Bit roomy for Siss and me but getting used to it. Sometimes she sits way down front, I in mezzanine, and we shout to each other when Gregory Peck does heroic things.

Collected first runs to add to *8½* from all major Manhattan houses—Capitol, Criterion, Cinema I & II, State, etc.—so we have good backlog. Also, if Siss likes, we run it again right away or next night. I don't mind. Then there are the 42nd St. houses and the art houses and the nabes & Mod. Museum film library. Shouldn't run out for a long time.

Days are for exploring and shopping. I go armed because of the animals. Siss stays home at hotel.

(*Why* are there animals? Find out. *Where* find out; how?)

The dogs in packs are worst. So far they haven't attacked and a shot fired in the air scares them off. So far.

Later they left the city. It had been too great a strain to live a life half primitive, half luxurious. The contrast was too much. And the rats were getting bolder. The rats and the dogs.

They had lived there at first for the convenience. He picked a hotel on Park Avenue. He put Siss in a single room and took a suite down the hall for himself.

He guessed correctly that there'd be huge refrigerators and freezers stocked with food enough for years.

The hotel, with its world-famous name, was one of the places the Consolidated Edison Company had boasted was on its Emergency Electricity net, along with City Hall, the Empire State Building, the tunnels and bridges, Governors Island and other key installations. The EE net, worked out for Civil Defense (what had ever become of Civil Defense?), guaranteed uninterrupted electricity to selected customers through the use of deep underground grids and conduits, despite flood, fire, pestilence or war. A promotional piece claimed that only total annihilation could knock out the system.

There was a hint of the way it worked in a slogan that Con Ed considered using before the government censors decided it would have given too much away: ". . . as long as the Hudson flows."

Whatever the secret, he and Siss had electricity, from which so many blessings flowed, for as long as they stayed in the city.

From his notebooks:

I've renamed our hotel The Living End. Siss calls it our house, or maybe Our House.

I won't let her go out by herself but she has the run of the hotel. She won't use the self-service elevators. Doesn't trust them. Don't blame her. She cooks in the hotel kitchen and carries our meals up two flights on a tray.

Garbage disposal no problem. There's an incinerator that must work by electricity. So far it's taken everything I've dumped down it. I can't feel any heat but it doesn't stink.

We're getting some outdoor stinks, though. Animal excrement that nobody cleans up (I'd be doing nothing else if I started). Uncollected garbage. Rotting food in supermarkets and other places without EE.

There are certain streets I avoid now. Whole sections, when the wind is wrong.

Bad night at the Living End. Had a nightmare.

I dreamed that Siss and I, home from the Music Hall (Cary Grant and Audrey Hepburn in something from the sixties), were having a fight. I don't know about what but we were shouting and I was calling her unforgivable names and she was saying she was going to climb up to the 20th floor and jump, when the phone rang . . .

I woke up, seeming to hear the echo of the last ring. The phone was there on the floor, under the night table.

I didn't dare pick it up.

It must have happened just before dawn, when Manhattan was as deserted as it ever got.

I took a chance on the EE and went up in the eleva-

tors to the top of the Empire State Bldg. First time I'd
ever been up—also the last, probably. What a sight.
Plenty of cars, cabs, trucks, buses rammed into each
other & sides of bldgs but lots more just came to nat-
ural(!) stop in midstreet or near curb. Very feasible to
drive around and out of town, tho probably not thru tunnels. GW Bridge shd be okay, with its 8 lanes. Have to
get out of town one day anyhow, so best explore in advance.

Planes. No sign that any crashed but bet lots did somewhere. Everything looks orderly at NY airports.

Fires. Few black spots—signs of recent fires. Nothing
major.

Harbor & rivers. Some ships, lots of boats drifting
around loose. No sign of collisions; nothing big capsized.

Animals. Dog packs here and there. Sound of their
barking rises high. *Nasty* sound. Birds, all kinds.

Air very dry.

Down in the street again, Rolfe began to think about
the animals other than the dogs that ran in packs. How
long would it be until the bigger ones—the wolves and
bears and mountain lions—found their way into the city?
He decided to visit Abercrombie & Fitch and arm himself
with something heavier than the pistol he carried. Big-
bore stuff, whatever they called it.

Rolfe was admiring an elephant gun in the fantastic
store (Hemingway had shopped here, and probably Martin and Osa Johnson and Frank Buck and others from
the lost past) when he remembered another sound he'd
heard from the top of the Empire State Building. It had
puzzled him, but now he could identify it. It had been the
trumpeting of an elephant. An elephant in Manhattan?
The circus wasn't in town— He knew then, but for the
moment he pushed aside the thought and its implications.

After he had picked out the guns, and a wicked gas-
operated underwater javelin for good measure, he outfit-
ted himself in safari clothes. Khaki shorts and high socks,

a big-pocketed bush jacket, a sun helmet. Hurrah for
Captain Spalding! He looked a true Marxman, he
thought, humming the song Groucho had sung and admiring himself in a full-length mirror.

He took a cartridge belt and boxes of shells and first-
aid and water-purification kits and a trapper's knife and a
light-weight trail ax and a compass and binoculars and
snowshoes and deerskin gloves and a tough pair of boots.
He staggered out into Madison Avenue and dumped
everything into the back of the cream-colored Lincoln
convertible he was driving that day.

The trumpeting of the elephant had come from the
Central Park Zoo, of course. He drove in from Fifth Avenue and parked near the restaurant opposite the sea lions'
pool. He could see three of them lying quietly on a stone
ledge, just above the water, watching him. He wondered
when they'd last been fed.

First, though, he went to the administration building
and let himself in with lock-picking tools. He had become
adept at the burglary trade. He found a set of what
seemed to be master keys and tried them first at the
aviary. They worked.

The names of the birds, on the faded wooden plaques,
were as colorful as their plumage. There were a Papuan
lory, a sulphur-crested cockatoo, the chiffchaff and kooka-
burra bird, laughing jackass and motmot, chachalaca,
drongo and poor old puffin. He opened their cages and
watched their tentative, gaudy passage to freedom.

A pelican waddled out comically, suspicion in its round
eyes. He ducked a hawk and cowered from a swift, fierce
eagle. An owl lingered, blinking, until he shooed it toward the doors. He left to the last two brooding vultures,
hesitating to free creatures so vile. But there was a role
for scavengers, too. He opened their cage and ran, to get
outdoors before they did.

After the cacophony of the aviary, he was surprised at
the silence as he neared the monkey house. He'd have to
be damned careful about the gorilla, which obviously had

to be shot. The big chimps were nothing to fool around with, either. But the monkey house was empty. The signs were there and the smell remained but the apes, big and little, were not. Could they have freed themselves? But all the cages were locked.

Puzzled, he went on to the smaller mammals, freeing the harmless ones, the raccoons, the mongooses, the deflowered skunks, the weasels and prairie dogs—even the spiny porcupine, which looked over its shoulder at him as it shuffled toward the doors.

He freed the foxes, too, and they bounded off as if to complete an interrupted mission. "Go get the rats," Rolfe yelled after them.

He marked the location of the wolves and the big cats. He'd come back to them with his guns.

Last of all he freed the lone elephant, scarcely grown, whose trumpet call had summoned him. The elephant— an unofficial sign said it was a female, Geraldine—followed him at a distance almost to the car, then broke into a clumsy trot and drank from the sea lions' pool.

As Rolfe was returning to the cages with the guns he knew why there weren't any monkeys. The big and little apes were hominids, like man. Their evolutionary climb had doomed them, too.

He killed the beasts of prey. It was an awful business. He was not a good shot even at close range and the executions took many bullets. A sinuous, snarling black panther took six before he was sure. The caged beasts, refusing to stand still for the mercy killings, made it hot, bloody, stinking work. He guessed it was necessary.

Finally he was done. Quivering and sweating, he returned to the car. The sea lions honked and swam across to his side of the pool. He could see now that there were three babies and two adults.

What was he to do with them? He couldn't bring himself to a final butchery. And what was he to do about all the other captive animals—in the Bronx Zoo uptown, in zoos all over the world? He couldn't be a one-man Animal Rescue League.

Rolfe had a momentary fantasy in which he enticed the sea lions into the car (four in the back, one in the front) and drove them to the East River, where they flopped into the water and swam toward the sea, honking with gratitude.

But he knew that in his present state of exhaustion he couldn't lift even the babies, and there was no way for them to get out of their enclosure unaided. Maybe he could come back with a truck and plank and fish to tempt them with. He left the problem, and that of the Bronx and Prospect Parks Zoos and the Aquarium (not to get too far afield) and started the car.

Geraldine looked after him. He would have liked a little trumpet of farewell but she had found some long grass and was eating.

As he drove back to the Living End through the wider streets, weaving carefully around the stalled cars, his mind was full of the other trapped beasts, great and small, starving and soon to go mad from thirst, as if in punishment for having outlived man.

Only then did the other thought crash into his consciousness—what of the millions of pets, trapped in the houses of their vanished owners? Dogs and cats, unable to open the refrigerators or the cans in the pantries. Some would have the craft to tear open packages of dried food and would learn to drink from leaking faucets or from toilet bowls. But at best they could prolong their miserable existence for only a few more days.

What was he to do about the pets? What could he do? Run around the city freeing them? Where would he start? Should he free all those on the north sides of odd-numbered streets? Or those on the ground floors of houses in named streets beginning with consonants? What were the rules? How did you play God?

He resolved not to talk to Siss about it. He wouldn't

have her breaking her heart over a billion doomed animals; she had enough to mourn.

From his notebooks:

What should I call today? Rolfeday? Sissuary the 13th? Year Zero?

Shd hav kept track but don't really know how many days it's been since I walked out of Bill's storage vault and found myself ½ the human pop. of the whole furshlugginer world.

Asked Siss. *She* remembers. It has been exactly 11 days since the holocaust. She accounted for every one of them. Moren I cld do: they started to run together for me after the first three.

OK, so it's Sissuary the 11th, Year One, Anno Rolfe. *Some*body's got to keep a record.

How many days in Sissuary? We'll see. Got to name the second month before closing out the first.

It was difficult for him to look back and remember exactly when he had first realized with certainty that this was the woman with whom he was fated to spend the rest of his life, when it had dawned on him that this moron was to be his bosom companion, that he had to take care of her, provide for her, *talk* to her (and *listen* to her), answer her stupid questions, *sleep* with her!

The realization must have come about the time he began to experience his stomach-aches. They weren't pains; they were more like a gnawing at the vitals of his well-being, a pincers movement by the enemy that was trapping him where he didn't want to be, with someone he didn't want to be with, a leaden weight that was smothering his freedom.

Some of her traits nearly drove him out of his mind. He was oversensitive, he supposed, but he had to wince and tried to close his ears every time she converted a sneeze into a clearly-enunciated "Ah *choo!*" and waited for him to bless her.

Worse because more frequent was her way of grunting audibly when she was picking up something, or pushing something or moving something around. This was to let him know that she was hard at work, for him. After a while he forced himself to praise her while she was at it —her diligence, her strength, her unselfishness—and she stopped making so much noise. He hated himself for being a hypocrite and felt sure she would see through him, but she never did and in the end his exaggerated praise became a way of life. It stood him in good stead later, when he had to tell her white lies about the degree of his affection for her and the great esteem in which he held her.

From his notebooks:

Asked Siss if she'd ever read a book and she said oh yes the Good Book. Parts of it. It used to comfort her a lot more in the old days, apparently. She's read two books all the way thru—Uncle Wiggily and Japanese Fairy Tales, and parts of a Tarzan book. She sometimes used to look at the paper—read the comics, the horoscope, picture captions, the TV listings. Lord save us from ever having to hold a literary conversation.

To be fair I've tried to remember the last 10 books I read before doom. Probably be a pretty stupid list if I was following my usual random reading pattern—off on an Erle Stanley Gardner or James Bond kick and reading everything available all at once.

Aside from his obligation to humanity to sire a new race, what was there for him to do? Rolfe considered the possibilities, dividing them into two groups: necessities (duties or obligations) and pastimes (including frivolities).

Under necessities he put:

Keep a journal for posterity, if any. He was already doing that.

Give Siss the equivalent of a grammar school education; more if she could take it.

Try to elevate her taste for the sake of the unborn children she would one day influence.

Keep his family fed and sheltered. Would it be necessary to clothe them, except for warmth in the winter? Nudity might be more practical, as well as healthier.

Then he jotted down on a separate piece of paper "Obligation to self paramount" and looked at it. He felt that he had to come first, with his duty to Siss a little lower (on the paper and in his estimation) because he was smarter than she was and therefore more worth saving.

Then he had another look and amended it. Siss was more worth saving because she was a woman and able to reproduce her kind.

But not without his help, of course.

Finally he put himself and Siss together at the top of the list. No good saving one without the other.

Pastimes. Take up a sport to keep fit. What one-man sports were there? Woodchopping? Fat chance. Too blister-prone, he. Hiking? Maybe he and Siss should hike around the world to make absolutely positively sure there was nobody else. Or around the eastern United States, anyhow. Or just up and down the Hudson River Valley? Somehow walking didn't seem to be his sport, either.

He might take up cooking. Men had always been the best chefs and now ingenuity would be needed to make nourishing and palatable meals from what was available to them. They couldn't depend on canned and preserved food forever. Okay, he'd be a cook. Of course that was a sport that tended to put pounds on, not take them off. He'd better find an antidote, like swimming or handball.

How about collecting? What—money? Diamonds? Great art? Neither money nor diamonds, obviously; neither had any intrinsic value in a World of Two—and then art was best left where it was, as well-protected as anything in the poor old world. If he wanted Siss to see a Rembrandt or an Andrew Wyeth, he'd take her to it.

From his notebooks:

Collecting old-fashioned windup phonographs against the day when no elec. Also old-fashioned 78 records. Got to keep so many things I can't reproduce.

Music. Good; Siss likes. She enjoys Tchaikowsky, Wagner and Beethoven (what wildness must stir within her poor head sometimes!) She'll sit still for Bach. I can't complain.

We're both crazy about Cole Porter, she for the music, I for the words, those great words, so much more ironic now than he had ever meant them to be.

"It's All Right With Me," for instance.

We've found a place. We—Is that the first time I've used the word?

It's far enough away from the city to be really country; beyond the stink and the reminders of dead glory; yet close enough so I can get in for supplies if I need them. I've stored up enough good gassed-up cars so that travel is no problem, but I think I'll try to stay here as much as I can. I used to be a fair woodsman. Let's see how much I remember.

It's peaceful here. My stomach-ache is better, all of a sudden.

He insisted on thinking of her as a person who had come into his custody and for whom he was responsible. For a long time all he felt toward her was pity; no desire. And for that reason he also pitied himself.

Because she was what she was, it would be unthinkable for her to touch him in any but the most innocent of ways, as she would one of her animal friends.

And when she called him anything but Mr. Ralph, using a word like honey, he was not flattered because he had heard her apply it also to a squirrel, a bluejay and a field mouse.

"Mr. Ralph, can I ask you a favor? Would you mind if you took me for a ride?"

It wasn't that she particularly wanted to go anywhere; apparently her enjoyment lay in sharing the front seat with him; he noticed that she sat very close to him, in almost the exact center of the seat and did not, as he had speculated she might, sit at the far right, next to the window.

For her ride she chose an ornate costume which included a hat, a silk scarf, dark glasses, jacket, blouse and skirt, stockings and half-heel shoes.

She picked the costume at what she called the Monkey Ward store while he shopped down the block for a fairly clean convertible with sound tires and a fair amount of gas in the tank.

They rode out past the quarry. Long ago he had stored away the fact that Quarry Road was the highway probably least littered with debris.

There was one bad place where he had to get off into a field to skirt what looked as if it had been a 50-car chain-reaction smashup. Otherwise, it was good driving all the way to the lake.

He parked near the old boat-launching site and automatically scanned the watery horizon for any sign of sail or smoke. He had never entirely abandoned hopes of finding other people.

He had brought from the liquor store (catty-corner from Monkey Ward's) a fifth of a high-priced Scotch and as they sat looking out over the lake he carefully opened it, preserving the tinfoil for her.

Then he ceremoniously offered her a drink. She declined, as he knew she would, saying:

"Not now, thanks. Maybe some other time." Apparently a piece of etiquette she'd learned was that it was bad manners to refuse anything outright—especially something to eat or drink.

Rolfe said: "I'll have one, though, if you don't mind."

And she replied, in what must have been a half-remembered witticism, "Take two, they're small."

He took two in succession, neither small.

The lake was serene, the sun was warm but not hot, a breeze blew from the east and the bugs were infrequent.

"Doesn't it bother you that there's nobody else?" he asked her. "Don't you get *lonesome?*"

But she said: "I'm always lonesome. I was. Now I'm less lonesome than I was. Thanks to you, Mr. Ralph."

Now what could he say to that? So he sat there, touched but scowling out at the horizon, and then he reached for the very old Scotch (the world had still lived when it was bottled) and took a very big swallow. Only later did he think to offer her one.

"Some other time, maybe," she said. "Not right now."

There came a day when her last brassiere lost its hooks and she obtained his dispensation to stop wearing it. And another when her blouses lost their buttons and refused to stay closed by the mere tucking of their tails into her skirts, and he told her it didn't matter in the least; until finally her last rags fell from her.

She said to him: "You're my Mr. Ralph, honey, and it's not wrong to be this way with you, is it, Mr. Ralph?"

This touched him so that he took her naked, innocent body in his arms and kissed the top of her clean, sweet head and he said:

"You're my big little girl and you couldn't do anything wrong if you tried."

And only then, for the first time, he felt a desire for this waif—this innocent in whom the seeds of the whole human race were locked.

She gave him a quick daring kiss on the cheek and ran off, saying: "It's time I started supper now. My gosh, we have to get you fed."

He remembered with shame a pathetic scene early in their life together. They had gone to Monkey Ward's and dressed from the skin out in brand-new evening clothes.

He'd had to help her cancel some tasteless combinations but at last she stood before him like an angel. Or, as he'd said: "Damned if you don't look like a Madison Avenue model."

"You shouldn't swear, Mr. Ralph," she'd said. "But thanks anyhow."

"And you shouldn't talk. You're welcome. Look, we're going to play a game. We're going to a fancy night club. We're going to make believe you're a mute—that you can't talk. No matter what, you must not say a word. Not a word."

"All right, Mr. Ralph."

"Starting right now, damn it! I'm sorry. I mean starting right now. All you can do is nod or smile. You can touch me if you want to. But you can't talk at all. That's part of the game. Do you understand?"

She started to say yes, then caught herself and nodded.

The silent nod from this beautifully gowned woman immediately made her ten times more attractive. Pleased with himself and with her, he gave her his arm and bowed her into the front seat of the Bentley he had searched out for their evening.

The night club had once been a major one, with a resident big-name band. Changing fashion had turned it into a discotheque, so that it had a juke box. He fed it a handful of coins to pay his way into a night of illusion. But the tables were bare and therefore wrong. He found a linen closet and set them with tableclothes and silverware, glasses, candlesticks.

The illusion grew. He found a switch that set in motion a set of colored lights which played on multi-faceted colored globes which hung from the ceiling. Another switch set them spinning slowly.

"What do you do in your spare time?" he asked her, knowing she wouldn't reply but wanting to see how she would react.

She shrugged, smiled a little and shook her head in

what he tried to imagine was an attitude that said she had so little spare time that it was negligible.

She was carrying out her part of the bargain. She did it extremely well. She listened without a word to his conversation, looking into his eyes as he pretended they were two among hundreds of elegant diners. He reconstructed talk from pre-holocaust nights out. He pretended she was a girl he had once been engaged to and told her extravagant things. She looked back at him and smiled, as if mockingly, as the old girl would have done. He pretended it was a later time, with the engagement in ruins and him solacing himself with the wife of his best friend, with the best friend's knowledge and consent, and the girl across from him gave him silent looks of profound sympathy. He pretended he had hired a call girl and spoke foully to her. She smiled bravely, her lips quivering, saying nothing.

Angered by the illusion which he had created and which mocked him, he drank too much and continued to abuse her—for herself, now; for doing as he had asked, for remaining silent.

The juke box was playing "Begin the Beguine" and ghostly dancers danced inside the circle of tables, under the soft colored lights. He saw them and cursed them for their nonexistence. He got up, knocking his chair over backwards, and shouted at her.

"Speak!" he said. "I release you from your muteness."

She shook her head, no longer smiling.

"Speak! you misbegotten halfwit! You monstrous bird-brained imposter! You scullery maid in a Schiaparelli gown. Speak, you—mental case."

But still she said nothing; merely looked at him with those deep eyes that seemed to understand and forgive.

Only at the very end of their evening out, when he had drunk himself into a stupor and stared across the room over her right shoulder, as if transfixed by his misery, did she speak. And then she said only:

"We better go home, Mr. Ralph, honey."

Then with a strength greater than his she half carried
him there to the car and drove him home and put him to
bed. It was a good thing he'd taught her to drive.

He woke up contrite, half remembering that he'd be-
haved unforgivably.

But she forgave him, as perhaps no one else ever
would have, using these words:

"I forgive you, Mr. Ralph. You knewd not what you
dood."

He was delighted. "Do not what I would," he said.
"Had I but dood what I could, who knew what would
have been dood?"

"I don't think that's very nice, Mr. Ralph. I said I forgive you. You're supposed to say thank you and say
you're sorry, even if you're not sorry."

He was still laughing at her, even after the realization
that he had a hangover.

"Okay. I'm sorry even if I'm not sorry and it's very
good of you to forgive me for my insufferable behavior,
even if nobody asked you to."

"Thank you for saying that, Mr. Ralph. Now I'll fix
you a hangover remedy."

"Where did you learn to concoct a hangover remedy,
for God's sake?"

"I was a working girl once for a poor man who got in-
toxicated and his wife. I learned it there."

She gave him no magic potion but an ordinary toma-
toey thing laced with pepper and Worcestershire sauce.
He drank it down but stubbornly declined to feel better
for a full hour. By then he had persuaded Siss he needed
a cold beer and she'd brought him one—disapproving but
proud of her ingenuity in having produced it, since they
kept no store of alcoholic beverages. She must have made
an ingenious search to find a cold beer; he was suddenly
proud of her.

But, remembering his performance of the night before,
he hated himself.

From the holding of hands to the kiss is not so far a thing as from the not holding of hands to the holding.

One thinks of the innocence of holding hands (children do it; men shake hands) but it is a vast journey from a platonic handclasp, over which there is no lingering, to the clasp which is so intense and telegraphic (accompanied, as it may be, by ardent gazing) that it would be a great surprise if the kiss to which it soon led were rebuffed.

And a kiss may lead anywhere. This he knew. He wondered how much she knew, or felt or surmised.

Dared he take her hand to help her across a stream or a rocky place? So far he had taken her arm, holding her firmly just above the elbow as if she were an elderly woman and he a large Boy Scout. He had no wish yet for anything more intimate.

It was a hesitant, tentative beginning to their romance.

"Do you mind my touching you?" he asked. Lately he had found that it gave him pleasure to touch her hair or trace the outline of her ear, or run his finger along her breastbone. Nothing carnal.

"No; I enjoy it."

And so they married. He arranged a ceremony, not only for her sense of propriety but to satisfy his demand for a kind of stability amid chaos.

He made it as elaborate as possible. He found a big flat rock to be the altar. He picked flowers and garlanded them into a headpiece for her. Let her head be covered, though her body was not.

She surprised him with a piece of writing. Crudely written in pencil on a sheet from a lined pad, it said:

"To my Mr. Ralph—

"This is our day to mary to-gether. My day and your day. I feel real good about it even if nobody else cant come. I'll try and make you a good wife with all my heart.

"I know you do the same thing for me because you are kind and good dear Mr. Ralph.

> "Your freind and wife
> · "Cecelia Beamer"

It was the first time he knew what Siss was the nick-name for.

Never before a sentimental man, Martin took his wife, Cecelia Beamer Rolfe, in his arms and kissed her with tenderness and affection.

He put her wedding-letter, as he thought of it, away in his desk, where it would be safe.

He wanted to consummate the marriage outdoors. It was a perfect June day, the sun warm, the grass soft, a breeze gentle. Lord knew they could not have asked for greater privacy than that of their own planet. But he felt Siss would have been, if not shocked, embarrassed unless four walls surrounded them.

Therefore he took her indoors, where she removed her flowery hat and put it in water, in a bowl.

Then she turned to him and said: "Tell me what to do, Mr. Ralph. I don't know what to do for you."

"For us, child," he said. "What we do—whatever we do from now on, is for us. Together."

"I like you saying that. Tell me what I should do."

"You don't have to do anything except be loved and love back in whatever way you feel. Anything you feel and do is right because you're my wife and I'm your hus-band."

"Would it be wrong for me to want you to hold me—here?" she asked. Eyes cast down, she touched her breasts. "I feel as if I'm bursting, I'm so full of love for my Mr. Ralph. I never thought—back then, that—"

He had to stop her talking and kissed her.

For a ring he had made a circlet of grass. When it broke apart or fell to pieces he made her another. In a way, he thought sometimes, it was like renewing the vows.

Once, years later, when he was looking for a pencil he found in the back of her drawer a collection of hundreds of wisps or strands of dried grass. She had saved each of the worn-out rings, obviously. She had kept them in a cheaply-manufactured container of plastic masquerading as leather which said in gaudy lettering "My Jewel Box." These were her gems, her only treasure.

He sometimes asked Siss, suddenly, intently: "Are you my friend?" And she would reply: "Yes, I am. Didn't you think so?" And he would be ashamed, but also gratified, and his heart would swell because she had said more than just Yes.

A woman is a race apart, a friend had told him once. "But," Rolfe added to himself, "this is ridiculous." He and Siss could not have been more unlike mentally.

Well, of course. That could have been true even if he'd had the whole world to choose from. Suppose she had been a selfish, empty-headed teenager; how long could he have stood someone like that? Or she could have been a crone, a hag; work-worn, fat, diseased, crippled. You're a pretty lucky guy, Martin Rolfe; Mr. Ralph, sir!

Sexually they were complementary, for instance. But was that enough? Except for little bits of time, no. But those are very important little bits of time, aren't they, Marty? Precious, even. Each a potential conception, a possible person.

But aside from that, no; it was not enough.

But because her entire existence was one of trying to please him, she learned eventually to make acceptable verbal responses and their mating became more satisfactory to him. His stomach ached less frequently.

By trial and error and by diligence, as she learned any task, she learned to speak to him in bed with an approximation of high intelligence, murmuring words of sympathy, approval, surprise, delight, playfulness, even shock at appropriate times. She learned to modulate her laughter, once coarse and raucous. She learned that a few words, sincerely but carefully expressed, did more for their mutual happiness than a babble, or an ungrammatical gush.

Her physical responses, as of a slave to a beloved master, had always been gratifying to him, except for her one unbreakable habit—her tendency to say "Oh, praise God!" whenever she achieved orgasm, or whenever she thought he had.

Once she had asked him to tell her about his life.

"What about it?" he had asked.

"All about it," she'd said.

"That would be a lot to tell."

"As much as you want to, then, Mr. Ralph."

Without a word of introduction he would start: "I was sixteen when I first kissed a girl. Awfully old . . ."

He'd always thought it shameful that he'd been unkissed so long and had never confessed it before. It was years later before Siss got up the courage to say: "Mr. Ralph, you told me once you didn't get a kiss till you were sixteen and that's too bad, but do you know how old I was?"

And he had said No, he didn't and she'd said:

"Twenty-eight, Mr. Ralph: that's how old. So don't you feel so bad."

And he'd asked her, though he was practically certain: "You mean I was the first one ever to kiss you?"

"The first man, except my father, yes, sir, Mr. Ralph. And do you know what? I'm awfully glad it was you that was the first, and that now nobody else ever will. I'm glad of that."

And so he had to postpone his confession. He had been on the point of telling Siss about his previous marriage—how he had chosen his wife from those available for matrimony among the fairly large number of women he had known.

What a fantastically wide choice he had had! The irony

of now, with no choice at all, made him marvel to think that he could have picked from among millions, had he known doom was to come and that he and his mate, if she too were saved, would be parents to the entire human race. With what care he would have searched, what exacting tests he would have applied, to screen the mass of womanhood for a fitting mate for the last man!

But because he had expected all life to continue he had chosen from an extremely small sample. Nevertheless he had chosen well.

Later he would tell Siss; not now. He would not hurt her at this time with talk about what, by hindsight, had been a perfect marriage; nor did he feel like hurting himself by contrasting a happy past marriage to an intelligent woman with what he had now.

Now he would tell Siss about another time in his adult past, a sad interlude during which he and his perfect wife had separated and he was living alone.

How foolish to have had that quarrel with his dead perfect wife, he thought. How senseless to have lost all the time that they might have had together.

Yet he had achieved a certain peace in his solitude. And their marriage had been stronger when he returned to her.

"I'm going to tell you about a time I was living all alone in a little trailer in the woods," he told Siss.

He had been a free-lance editor in those days, doctoring doddering magazines, doing articles for his editor friends, and reading for a publishing house, and so was able to avoid the frenzied daily commute. He used the mails and phone and got into the city a couple of times a month.

He enjoyed an occasional dinner or cocktail party in his exurb; but he valued his privacy enough to decline many invitations and to withdraw to his trailer.

Rolfe himself never entertained. His truck-back trailer home was unsuited for anything but the shortest of visits. He'd have the mailman in for a drink of Bourbon on

Christmas Eve, or chat with the man who came around to collect for the volunteer ambulance corps, or play ten-second-move chess with the route man who delivered the only food Rolfe ate at home—eggs, and the butter he fried them in.

The truck-back home normally sat in the middle of Rolfe's eighteen acres—far enough out of town so that there were woods to surround him and a dammed-up stream in which to swim, but close enough for an electric power line to be run in.

If Rolfe's choice of this way to live during his separation was an eccentricity, then he was eccentric. One other thing about him was a little odd. He had nailed a sign to a tree at the beginning of the track which led off the county road to his place. It said:

PRIVATE ROAD
MINED

The police came around after he put up the sign, which he'd burned into the end of an egg crate with an electric pen. The policemen, a lieutenant and a sergeant, left their car at the county road and walked carefully along the edge of Rolfe's track to the pickup truck in the clearing near the dammed-up stream. A pheasant moved without haste into some undergrowth as they came up to the door over the tailgate.

Rolfe invited them in, making room for them to sit down by lifting a manuscript off the one easy chair and motioning the sergeant to the camp chair in front of the typewriter on the bracket that folded down from the wall. Rolfe sat on the single bunk along the driver's side, having first got cokes out of the tiny refrigerator. He knew better than to offer liquor to policemen on duty. They chatted for a while before the lieutenant said: "About your sign, Mr. Rolfe; we've had some complaints."

"Call me Martin. Complaints? I like my privacy, that's all."

"My name's Sol," the lieutenant said, "and this is Eric." They shook hands all round again, now that the first-name basis had been established, and Sol said: "About the road being mined. Sure it's private property and nobody respects the principle of that more than I do, but somebody might get hurt. Somebody who couldn't read, maybe, or who wandered in after dark—not really meaning to trespass, you know."

"Sure," Rolfe said. "I can understand that."

"Besides," the sergeant—Eric—said, "anybody with war surplus ammunition was supposed to have turned it in years ago. It's the law."

"I don't know what you mean," Rolfe said. "I haven't booby-trapped the road. I wouldn't hurt a rabbit, much less a human being. Why, I'm so soft-hearted I don't even fish the stream."

Sol said: "I get it. You just put up the sign to keep people away—like 'Beware of the Dog,' even if you don't have a dog."

"And there really aren't any bouncing Bettys out there then?" Eric said. "I'm relieved. Believe me, we walked mighty easy along the edge."

Martin Rolfe grinned. "Gentlemen, I think I begin to understand. And it's all my fault because I'm such a poor speller. What I was trying to do was to call attention to the fact that it isn't a public road or a hiking trail or a place for young vandals to go if they have a hankering to break windows or set fires in out-of-the-way places. I believe there've been a few such incidents around town."

"Too many," Sol said. "But I still don't know what you mean about being a poor speller."

"What I intended to say on the sign, I guess, was 'Mind you, this is a private road.' It's a kind of New England expression."

"I've heard it," Eric said. "They have signs like that in London, where my wife's from—she was a war bride, you know, Lieutenant—that say 'Mind the step.'"

"That's m-i-n-d, not m-i-n-e-d," Sol said.

"Is that right?" Rolfe asked with a grin. "I told you I wasn't much of a speller. I'd better change the sign, then, hadn't I?"

Instead of replying directly, Sol asked: "Ever have trouble with kids back in here?"

"Kids and grown-ups both," Rolfe said. "Different kinds of trouble. Kids broke a window one night. I was asleep and got a shower of broken glass all over my face. Another time a big brave man with a gun shot the hell out of a mother partridge and her brood and left them flopping around. He wasn't even planning to eat them. Did you ever put a living thing out of its misery with your bare hands, Sol? That same day I put up the sign. The partridges and I haven't been bothered since."

Sol got up and let himself out into the clearing. "I had to kill a doe once that some mighty hunter put a hole into but didn't think worth following into the brush." Eric went out with Martin Rolfe behind him and all three walked along the middle of the track to the county road. Birds chirped at them and a leisurely rabbit hopped away.

At the blacktopped road Martin Rolfe went to his sign. He took a pencil out of his shirt pocket and scratched a vertical line through the *E* in *mined*. Then he joined the *N* and *D* with a copyreader's mark.

The sergeant said, "I don't know that that's too highly visible. Besides, a couple of rains'll wash it off."

"Oh, come on, Eric," the lieutenant said, getting into the car. "It's as plain as day."

"Thanks, lieutenant," Martin said, going over to the police car to say goodbye. "I never could spell worth a damn."

"Oh, yeah?" Eric said. "I'll bet you can outspell both of us any day." He was looking back at the sign as he got into the car and he tripped, so that he had to grab for the door to steady himself.

"Mind the step," Martin said.

It was achingly poignant for him to leaf through the pages of a copy he'd saved of *The New York Times Magazine*.

How lovable and childlike seemed the people doing the weird things fashion advertising demanded of them! How earnest were the statements made in the articles and the letter pages. For example, there was the ironic, the heartbreakingly laughable article about the population explosion—about the insupportable hundreds of millions there soon would be in India, or the six billion there'd be on Earth in just a few more years.

Would that there were only as many people as had read that particular Sunday issue of the *Times*. A million and a half? World enough. Or even if there existed on Earth only the few hundred people it had taken to write, edit and print that particular issue of *The New York Times Magazine*. Even if there were only *one* other than Siss and himself. One man to play chess with, or to philosophize with.

He thrust away from him the thought that the third person on Earth might be another woman. It was too dangerous, too explosive a thought. Would he betray Siss for a normal woman? Certainly he would never abandon her, but betrayal was certain—she would be so easy to fool. What form, other than an intellectual one, would it take? Would he take the new woman blatantly as his mate, with a facile explanation to Siss? Would the new one try to banish Siss (he'd never stand for that—would he?), or decree a demeaning role for her in a reorganized household—something he might rationalize himself into accepting? (He could hear the new one saying: "You want our children—Earth's only children—to be intelligent, don't you? You don't want the new world peopled with feeble-minded brats, do you?")

His thoughts went back to the possible consequences if a third person were male. Suppose the man were not a chess player? Suppose he were a mere brute, with brutish instincts? Would Martin have to share Siss with him, Eskimo style? Even if he could bring himself (or Siss) to accept such an arrangement, how long could it continue without an explosion?

No—as long as he was fantasizing it would be simpler to dream up two other people, a man and a woman who had already arranged their own lives, who had made the adjustment.

Still—how long could two couples—and only two— live side by side without something boiling over? Wife-swapping was too prevalent an institution in the bad old days, when there was all kinds of other entertainment, not to be a daily temptation in an all-but-depopulated world.

No—it would be best to have no third or fourth person —not unless there could be an infinity of others besides . . .

Ah, but he was so *lonely!*

"I'm going to the city," he told Siss.

They had done without the city for a long time. They had made do with the things they had, or could make; they'd let their clothing drop away and hadn't replaced it; they'd grown their own food; made their country house the center of their universe. But now he wanted to go back.

She must have seen something in his eyes. "Let me go for you," she said. "Just tell me what you want."

Sometimes she chose such an ironic way of saying things that he fleetingly suspected her of having not only intelligence but wit.

"Just tell you what I want! As if—" He stopped. As if he could tell her. As if he knew.

He knew only that he had to get away for a little while. He wanted to be alone, with his own memories of a populated Earth.

He also wanted a drink.

Long ago he had made it a rule never to have liquor in the house. It would be too great a temptation to have it handy. He could see himself degenerating into a drunken bum. With an unlimited supply close at hand and a devoted woman to do all the work that needed to be done, he could easily slip into an animalistic role—become a creature with a whiskey-sodden, atrophied brain.

A fitting father and mother to the world such a pair would be!

And so he had made his rule: drink all you want when you have to—in the city—but never bring it home.

And so he had told Siss: "I don't know what I want, exactly. I just want to go to the city."

And she had said: "All right, Mr. Ralph, if you have to."

There was her perception again, if that's what it was. "If you have to," she'd said, though he'd talked of want, not need.

"I do," he said. "But I'll come back. Is there anything I can bring you?" She looked around the kitchen and began to say something, then stopped and said instead: "Nothing we really need. You just go, Mr. Ralph, and take as long as you have to. It'll give me a chance to go do that berry-picking I been wanting to."

She was so sweet that he almost decided not to go. But then he kissed her—very thankful, just then, that she was his Siss and not some too-bright shrew of a problem wife —and went. He drove in, naked in a Cadillac.

He had rolled the swivel chair out of the store onto the sidewalk and was sitting in it in the afternoon sunshine. Beside him on the pavement were half a dozen bottles, each uncapped. He was talking to himself.

"As the afternoon sun, blood-red through the haze of the remnants of a once overpopulated world, imperceptibly glides to its bed, one of the two known survivors becomes quietly plastered." He had a drink on that, then went on:

"What thoughts pass through the mind of this pitiful creature, this naked relic of a man left to eke out the rest of his days on a ruined planet?

"Does he ever recall the glory that once was his and

that of his fellows? Or is he so sunk in misery—in the mere scratching of a bare existence from an arid soil—that he has forgotten the heights to which his kind once had risen? Subject pauses in thought and reaches for bottle. Drinks deeply from bottle, but not so deeply as to induce drunken sickenness. Aim of subject is quiet plasterization, happy drunkdom, a nonceness of Nirvana, with harm to none and bitterness never. Sicken drunkenness?

"A respite of reverie, perhaps, as subject casts mind back to happy past. Mr. Martin Rolfe in Happier Days."

He picked up his *New York Times Magazine* and leafed through it. It was almost as good as having another drink. There they were—they couldn't have been more than 17 —leaping in their panty girdles to show the freedom of action and the elasticity of the crotch. He remembered once having heard a newsman, waiting in the rain for the arrival of a President, say: "Being a reporter is essentially an undignified occupation." So had been being a model, obviously.

Things of the past . . . He thought: "A title for my memoirs—*Things of the Past*." He took up the *Times* again and turned to an ad of a debonair young man in a revolving door holding a copy of the *Wall Street Journal*. "I dreamt I was trapped in a revolving door in my Arcticweave tropical worsted," Rolfe said, summing up the situation. He looked like the 28-year-old Larchmont type; five years out of college, with a Master's, two kids, wife beginning to drink a little bit too much. "If he's trapped there long enough he may read the paper right through to the shipping pages and ship out to the islands."

Rolfe looked pityingly at the trapped Larchmont type, armed against his predicament only with his Arcticweave suit, his *Wall Street Journal* and, presumably, a wallet full of wife-and-baby pictures, credit cards and a commutation ticket issued by a railroad company petitioning to suspend passenger service.

"You poor bastard," Rolfe said.

Of course he was saying it to himself, too. He said it

all the way home: "You poor bastard. You poor bastard."

Siss was waiting for him in the cool garden. Gently she led him indoors. She said, with only the slightest hint of reproach (he could stand that much—he deserved more): "You been drinking too much again, Mr. Ralph. You know it's bad for you."

"You're right, Siss. Absolutely right."

"You got to take care of yourself. I try to, but you got to try, too."

Tenderly she put him to bed. He knew then, among other times, how much he needed her, and he struggled to say something nice to her before he dropped off to sleep. Finally he said: "You know, Siss, you're nicer than all those crazy leaping girls in the York Times." That's what she called it, the York Times. "You got a lot more sense, too, than they look as if they had."

From his notebooks:

Got drunk saft. Downtown. Dangerous. Not fair to Siss. Liable get et up by dogs while stinko. Bad show.

Can't bring bottle home, tho. Too great a temptation to get sozzled daily and twice on Sunday.

Why is Sunday worse than other days? I tried to rename it but Siss insisted we keep it. She also demanded it come every seven days, just like in good old days. Had to give in. So much for calendar reform.

He sought other ways of escaping. He hiked and climbed and explored.

Once he found a spot on the brow of a hill from which one (that is, he) could see for miles but from which no work of man was visible except the top of a silo at the top of a similar hill across a wide valley.

Having found the spot, he cleared wild strawberry plants from beneath a young maple tree, leaving the ferns and the cushiony moss, and lay down to rest. It had been a strenuous climb, and hot, and now the insects were upon him. But though the flies buzzed they did not often land and the mosquitoes were torpid and easily slapped. After a while—it was almost noon (as if the hour mattered)—he had a couple of swallows from the flask he carried in his rucksack and ate some cheese. He thought of the flask as his iron rations.

As he rummaged in the rucksack he found a roll of plastic tape he'd brought along to help him blaze a trail. He hadn't needed it; instead he'd marked his way by cutting branches with a long-handled pruning tool.

But as he lay in the solitude he had sought out and found (how odd to seek solitude in an empty world!), under one of a myriad of trees, where the only sounds were of buzzing insects, chirping birds, the soughing of trees in a soft wind—he knew what to do with the plastic tape. He printed something on a little square of paper, small but legible, and, with the tape, attached it to the lowest bough of his young maple. Now he lay under it, savoring what he had done.

The little sign said: THIS TREE RESERVED.

One June night it rained in great, warm, wind-driven sheets. He had not experienced such a storm since a visit a decade earlier to the tropics.

The pleasure he took in the soaking, bath-temperature rain was enhanced by the danger from the lightning. It stabbed down from the sky as if seeking him out, destroying and burning only yards away, as if it would be a great cosmic joke to strike that one spot on the surface of the Earth and kill the last man.

He defied it, prancing wildly, then halting deliberately as if transfixed when it flashed, posing with outthrust or upthrust arms, yelling, defying the thing or Being that had sent the storm, loosing his pent-up frustrations, his disappointments and hates in the elemental power of the storm.

He had trapped the beast in a pit, unfairly. It had

nearly exhausted itself in attempts to leap the sheer walls. At least he hadn't lined the bottom with spikes.

Rolfe could have killed it from above, poisoned it, let it starve. Instead he jumped into the pit, armed with two knives, to risk mauling and death.

He realized his folly instantly. The creature was far from helpless. Its claws were sharp, though its movements were clumsy in the cramped pit-bottom, and its fetid breath was as much a weapon as its fangs.

Only by the sheerest of luck, he felt, did he avoid the claws and fangs long enough to plunge first one knife then the other into the beast's heart.

As its death struggles subsided he lay there, his face buried in the back of its neck, hugging the thing he'd killed, a sadness coming over him as he felt the fading heartbeat.

Later he skinned the beast. He and Siss ate the meat and slept under the pelt. But first he had buried the head, in tribute to a worthy antagonist, a kind of salute to another male.

And unto them was born a son.

Siss seemed to know just what to do, by instinct. Clumsily he helped. He cut the umbilical with a boiled pair of scissors. Made a knot. Washed the red little thing.

Eventually Siss lay quiet, dry, serene, holding her swaddled child. He sat on the floor next to the bed and looked and looked at the mother and child. A holy picture, he thought. He sat for hours, staring, wondering. She looked back at him, silent, wondering.

The new human being slept, serene.

It could not have been more perfect.

His son. His boy. His and hers but, he felt it fair enough to say, mostly his.

His son Adam. What else had there been to name him? Adam. Trite but noble. He had considered calling him Ralph, but only briefly. It would be too comical to have his mother go around introducing him to their near circle of friends—relatives all, come to think of it—as Ralph Ralph.

There'd be no need for introductions for many years, of course, in a closed society such as theirs. The years did pass.

There was his son, tall for his age, straight, brown, good with his hands . . .

But bright? Intelligent? How was a father to know? A prejudiced parent sees only the good, ignores what he doesn't want to accept, can be oblivious to faults obvious to anyone else.

He talked to him and got gratifying responses. But wouldn't almost any response be gratifying to a parent? Parents are easily satisfied. Especially fathers of sons.

Had he conditioned himself to the point where he would be satisfied if his son showed more than animal intelligence? The conditioning encompassed an agony of watching as his son grew—watching for signs of mental retardation, of idiocy, of dullness, or bigheadedness, of torpor.

And then they had a daughter.

From his notebooks:

My son. Brown as a penny. Naked as a jaybird. Slender, muscled, handsome, active, good with his hands.

Bright? Seems so. Obviously too soon to really tell.

Five years old and just made his first kill. Wild dog, attacking our goat. Got him in the right eye with a .30-30 at_____yards (measure and fill in).

Strong and brave and skilled and good looking.

Let's hope intelligent, too.

Please, God.

My daughter. My precious, my beauty. What a delight you are, with your serene smile and your loving way of wrapping your arms around my leg and looking up at Old Daddy. You're your mother's child, aren't you? So good, so quiet. But you're quick on your feet and your reflexes (I've tested them) are sound. I think we're all right.

The Diary of Siss

(Siss was not very faithful about her diary. The printed word was not her medium. Although her intentions were obviously good, there are fewer than a dozen entries in all, and they are reproduced below. She did not date them. The handwriting in the last entry is slightly better than that of the first, but maybe only because she was using a sharper pencil. A more revealing diary probably would be found in her heart, if that could be read, or in her children.)

Mr. Ralph told me write things down when they big & inportant I will start now. Today Mr. Ralph married me.

Very happy today. Learning to please my husband.

_____

Very very happy. Today moved to our country house I like it better than the big city.

_____

Today I had a baby, a boy.

_____

My word for today is contentment. I have to spell it and tell what it means. Mr. Ralph says I need an eddukaton, he will eddukate me.

_____

My word for today is education. Mr. Ralph seen what I wrote in my dairy yestdy.

_____

I have 2 words for today diary & yesterday. Also saw not seen.

Today I had a baby, a girl. Ralph said now everything is going to be alright.

And presumably it was. Having doubled the population, the human race seemed to be on a firm footing. There was love in the world; a growing, proud family, and a new self-assurance in Siss—note that he was Ralph now, not Mr. Ralph. We may be sure, though, that the strict if loving father gave her two words for tomorrow: all right. A father, a mother, a son, a daughter. A little learning, a lot of love.

In the summer of his eighth year Adam and his father were in the woods back of the pasture, in the little clearing at the side of the stream that ran pure and sparkling before it broadened into the shallow muddy pond the livestock used. Martin and the boy were eating lunch after a morning of woodcutting and conversation.

Adam, naked like his father, had asked: "Am I going to grow some more hair, like you?"

And Martin said: "Sure, when you get bigger. When you begin to be a man."

And Adam had compared his smooth skin with his father's hard, muscled, hairy body and said: "Mom's got hair in that place, too, but she's different."

So Martin explained, sweating even though he was sitting still now, and his son took it all in, nodding, just as if it were no more important than knowing why the cow had her calf. It was obvious that until now Adam had not connected the function of the bull with the dropping of the calf. Martin explained, in human terms.

"That's pretty neat," Adam said. "When do I get to do it?"

Martin tried to keep his voice matter-of-fact. How do you instruct your son in incest?

The explanation was completed, finally, and it was Martin's turn to ask a question. "Think carefully about this, son. If you could save the life of one person—your mother or me but not the other—which would you save?"

Adam answered without hesitation. "I'd save Mother, of course."

Martin looked hard at his strong, handsome son and asked the second part of the question. "Why?"

Adam said: "I didn't mean to hurt your feelings, Dad. I'd save both of you if I could—"

"I know you would. You've been a crack shot since you were five. But there might be only one chance. Your answer is the only possible one, but I have to know why you gave it."

The boy frowned as he struggled to reason out the reply he had made instinctively. "Because—if necessary —she and I could—" Then it came out in a rush: "Because she could be the mother to the world and I could be the father."

Martin shuddered as if a long chill had just passed. It was all right. He embraced his fine, strong, *intelligent* son and wept.

After a little while Siss appeared, walking the path beside the stream, naked as the two of them but different, as Adam had said, and riding the naked baby on her hip.

"Thought we'd join the menfolks for lunch," she said. "I picked some berries for dessert." She carried the blackberries in a mesh bag and some had been bruised, staining the tanned skin a delicate blue just below her slim waist.

Martin said: "You sure make a good-looking picture, you two. Come here and give me a kiss."

The baby kissed him first, then toddled off to smooch up for Adam, who gave her a dutiful peck.

Their father held open his arms and Siss sat beside him, putting the berries aside. She rested her head on his shoulder, serene. Martin folded her to him and kissed her eyes and cheeks and hair and neck and finally her lips, there in the sunshine, by the side of the pure stream, in the presence of all the world.

"Do you think—" she started to say, but Martin said "Hush, now. It's all right. Everything's all right, Siss darling." She sighed and relaxed against him. He had never called her darling before. He kissed her again for a long time and she gradually lay back on the soft ground and raised one knee and bent the other to accommodate her husband.

The baby lost interest and went to wade in the stream but Adam watched, his elbow on his knee, and once he said, "Don't crush the blackberries," and reached out to get them. He ate a handful, slowly.

Then he heard his mother gasp, "Oh, praise God!" and after a moment both his parents became still. And after a little while longer he looked to see that the baby was okay and then went to the intertwined, gently-breathing bodies, which were more beautiful than anything he had ever seen.

Adam knelt beside them and kissed his father's neck and his mother's lips. Siss opened her arms and enfolded her son, too.

And Adam asked, with his face against his mother's cheek, which was wet and warm, "Is this what love is?"

And his mother answered, "Yes, honey," and his father said, in a muffled kind of way, "It's everything there is, son."

Adam reached out for the berries and put one in his mother's mouth and one in his father's and one in his. Then he got up to give one to the baby.

In Orbit 1, *it was "The Secret Place"; in* Orbit 2, *"Fiddler's Green." Now here is "Bramble Bush," and it is the last. After this, there will be no more stories by Richard McKenna in* Orbit.

This remarkable story was written early in McKenna's career: he brought it to the Milford Writers' Conference in 1960 or thereabouts. I did not understand a word of it then, and concluded that it was a failure. After McKenna's death in 1964, it turned up in a batch of manuscripts Eva McKenna sent me. Reading it again, with more care, I discovered that far from being muddled all the way through, it was a brilliant and perfectly lucid story, buried under a mass of trivial confusions inadvertently or deliberately introduced by the author. With Mrs. McKenna's permission, therefore, I made a number of minor changes, mostly in the characters' names. (In the original version, half a dozen of the characters had names that looked or sounded alike.) Except for these, the story remains as McKenna wrote it. It is that rare thing, a pure science fiction story. It deals with one of the most puzzling questions in relativity, one to which Einstein never gave an unequivocal answer: If all four spacetime dimensions are equivalent, how is it that we perceive one so differently from the rest?

Only a writer with McKenna's peculiar talents and training could have given this solution, which involves the anatomy of the nervous system, symbology, anthropology, the psychology of perception . . . and magic.

Bramble Bush

by Richard McKenna

Team Leader Ed Gard did not tell them until after Explorer Vessel M-24 rotated irreversibly into subspace.

"We'll not come out by kappa-12 Carinae," he said then to the five men standing clumped in the control room. "We're going to alpha-1 Centauri."

Fat Webb Onderdonck, the climatologist, exploded. "A field trip for kids! How come?"

"Isn't it already settled?" asked Minelli, the slender geologist.

Shipman Isaac McPherson punched a reference combination and glanced at the lighted screen.

"One Earth-type planet named Proteus," he said, frowning. "Never been a landing. Now why didn't I ever wonder about that before? My God, the nearest system to Earth—"

"Only in the Riemannian sense," Onderdonck broke in. "Means nothing relative to subspace." McPherson's craggy face cleared.

"But we've taken them in order of Riemannian contiguity all along," objected Chalmers, the biochemist. "This exception does seem unaccountable. There *must* be a reason." His thin, sharp features were troubled.

"Overlooked in the shuffle. Maybe a misfiled report. What's one planet anyway, among a billion?" Webb Onderdonck scowled.

"Not so, Webb," Gard said, squaring massive shoulders. "In the past century the Corps projected several trips to Proteus. Each one aborted through a long series of personnel accidents and other delays. We are the first to get away."

"Why the secrecy? Who's being fooled?"

"Fate, maybe. A sop to superstition. Sit down, people, and I'll explain."

Seated along the wall bench, all but the scowling fat man, they listened as their tall leader paced and talked. Proteus had been his personal mystery since he was ten years old, he said, and the mystery was that no one else was curious.

"Everybody shushed my questions and got mad when I persisted," he said. "Just one of those things, they kept telling me, too many planets to worry about any single one. It came to me that the most insoluble mystery is one that no one will admit exists."

He aimed his education at the Explorer Corps, he went on, enlisted and in time qualified as team leader. When he tried to rouse official interest in a trip to Proteus he hit a stone wall of indifference grading into covert hostility. But finally he had infected Vane, the project coordinator at Denverport, with his own curiosity. Together they had planned this secret diversion of a routine Carina trip.

"So here we go, people. Don't all hate me at once." He put up his hands in mock-guard.

"Curiosity killed a cat," Onderdonck snorted, jowls quivering. "Your mystery is childish nonsense. This will finish you in the Corps, and Vane too."

"*How* did curiosity kill the cat?" Hank Chalmers asked. "I don't like this either, Webb, but I can't put my finger on a reason."

"A planet's a planet, all in the day's work," Minelli soothed. "Let's do a job on this Proteus and there'll be no more mystery."

Joe Svirsky, the biologist, stood up. He was a stocky, graying man with cheekbones prominent in a broad face under slanting gray eyes.

"This is no ordinary mission, my brothers," he said gravely. "We must be careful."

"Amen to that," Gard grinned. "Afterward let the Corps bounce me as far as it likes. I've been pointing for this all my life."

Proteus circled the smaller star close in. Its day was fourteen standard hours, no axial tilt and so no seasons, gravity point seven, air breathable but hot and humid, the instruments told them. Gard called a pre-landing conference in the main workroom on their second day in orbit.

"Mean relief under ninety feet. Eighty-five percent sea, most of it epeiric. Never saw an Earth-type so leveled off," Minelli said.

"Mean annual temperature estimate twenty degrees above optimum," Onderdonck said, looking at Gard across the table. "That alone rules out settlement. No landing necessary now or ever and pop goes your mystery. Let's go home."

"We must sample the biota for a complete report," Gard disagreed. "We serve man's land hunger *and* his curiosity."

"Speak for yourself!" Onderdonck snapped, rising and propping himself on pudgy fingers. "I invoke article ten of regulations and call for a vote of supersession."

"Hold on, Webb, that makes bad feeling," Pete Minelli said. "Besides, I want a closer look at that textbook peneplain down below."

Onderdonck insisted. Only Chalmers, glancing apologetically at Gard, voted with him.

"Take her down, Ike, the place Minelli picked," Gard told the shipman.

McPherson set her down on a continental dome, a comparatively well-drained area of grassy swales and broad-leaf tree clumps.

"Looks ordinary as hell," McPherson said, standing at the foot of the ramp.

"Hot as hell too," Minelli said. "Steam bath. Me for swimming trunks." He started back aboard.

"Just a minute, Pete," Gard called after him. "I was about to propose we stay on ship-time on account of the short local day. Okay with you?"

"Hell yes, what's time to a geologist?"

They agreed to stay on ship-time. Svirsky was already taking soil and water specimens from a sluggish stream nearby. Chalmers gathered grass seeds and berries.

"Help with the biota, Webb, and we'll do a minimal job, get out fast," Gard offered.

"No," Onderdonck growled, "and don't figure on that account I'll take galley duty, either."

Gard shrugged his broad shoulders.

Chalmers started on protein analysis and Svirsky on the microbiota. Gard, McPherson and Minelli set up observation units in the few varying habitats the gray-green flatness afforded on a five-mile radius from the ship. Each unit transmitted to a scope on the monitor panel in the main workroom and could be switched at will to the large stereo-screen. The three men took turns on monitor watch, making selective recordings of animal behavior for later analysis.

Native protein was unusually similar to that of Earth. The native vertebrates were Earth-homologous too, including birds and reptiles, but small. The largest land animal seemed to be a goat-sized herbivore. Svirsky turned to a comparative anatomy series and Gard and the shipman trapped specimens for him when off watch. Minelli ranged afield in the atmospheric flyer for geology specimens. Outside the ship the men wore swimming trunks and cursed the heat. After two standard weeks Gard tentatively decided to lift out on the following day.

That afternoon Pete Minelli burst into the main workroom shouting, "Ed, hey Ed, there's men on this planet!"

Svirsky turned sharply from his dissecting table. Chalmers came in from his lab across the passageway, pale and staring. McPherson, at the monitor panel, tugged at his red mustache and Onderdonck flushed. Gard spoke for them all.

"Pete, you're crazy with the heat! What do you mean?"

"At least one man, by God!" Minelli insisted. "Big as you and red-headed as Ike over there. Naked and bearded and wild."

"Tell us about it. Did you speak to him?"

"I was taking a core not far from here and this fellow was all of a sudden there, walking sideways around me with a stupid look on what I could see of his face. It shook me up, Ed. All I could think to do was keep turning to face him. After about three laps he went into the brush and I got out so fast I left my drill rig there."

"Somebody marooned? Maybe a lost Earth colony?" McPherson wondered, rubbing his long chin.

"Could be native," Gard murmured.

"I'll be damned," McPherson said. "Everybody knows men are unique to Earth. We haven't found humans on ten thousand planets now."

"We've found bipedal mammals on plenty of them. These could easily be human-homologs. Right, Joe?"

Svirsky nodded gravely, his eyes wide.

"If so, it's contact," Onderdonck said thickly. "Gard, you fool, you've found man's first rival for the galaxy. You *would* persist!"

"Hey, here's one come into a scope!" McPherson shouted. "I'll switch it over."

A scene of brown-flowered grass and gray-green shrubs took shape in the big stereo. A naked woman squatted, partially covered by long, coppery hair, and plucked grass racemes which she ate or fed to a scrabbling infant beside her.

"Who's crazy now?" Minelli asked, looking around the group. "Ike, there's a carrot-top soulmate for you."

The woman suddenly looked directly out of the screen. Her heavy features were expressionless, her slaty eyes dull.

"Opposites attract," McPherson retorted. "Pete, she's giving you the eye."

"Not a very bright eye," Gard said. "They're not exactly potent rivals, Webb."

The woman shambled off the screen, eating as she went, the child scrabbling after. McPherson worked his controls.

"Here, I got 'em on another one," he said. "Hey! there's a man!"

The man was eating one of the goat-things. It twitched and jerked with residual life. The woman joined him in gnawing at it. From time to time she fed partially chewed flank muscle to the infant.

"Hell, they must be native," McPherson said disgustedly. "No human could slide back that far."

"Gard, let's get out of here fast," Hank Chalmers said abruptly.

"Not till I try communication."

"Obviously useless. They're pure animal, for all their shape."

"Hank, you know better than that. Extrapolate from that otter-homolog Joe has on his table. These Proteans must have a nervous system capable of forming a very rich symbol world. Right, Joe?"

"Yes, but unlike the skeleton and musculature it is Earth-anomalous," Svirsky said. "The pyramidal motor tracts in the cord do not cross. It might be a very strange symbol world."

"In what way?"

"We don't care!" Onderdonck burst out. "This is a waste of time on an unauthorized deviation from assigned mission. I vote to supersede Gard and go home. Who's with me?"

"I am," Chalmers muttered, casting down his eyes.

"Damn it, Ed, I want to back you, but set *some* limit," Minelli pleaded.

"Okay, Pete, a time limit. Give me one standard week."

"Okay, a week. I'll ride along."

"Me too," McPherson said. Svirsky nodded agreement.

Over the next three days Proteans by the score came into the observation area, circling aimlessly to within a mile of the ship. They fled when Gard approached them in the field, doubling back to their dumb circling of him when he stood still. He developed headaches and overpowering fits of lethargy and suspected a virus, but Chalmers' bio-analyzer found no foreign protein in him. Frequently McPherson and Minelli watched his maneuverings on the scopes and twitted him later.

"You're too hoity-toity, Ed," McPherson said. "Squat down and eat snakes with 'em and they'll trust you."

"If you'd grow a beard, Ike, they'd make *you* a chief," Gard grinned.

On the morning of his fourth day in the field Gard woke in confusion on a grassy bank. McPherson and Minelli were bending over him and his left shoulder ached horribly.

"She was eating me," he said stupidly.

"Yes," Minelli agreed, white-faced. "You just folded up. Lucky we were watching. Lucky nobody had the flyer out."

"Get aboard, get aboard," McPherson urged. "That shoulder needs fixing."

Chalmers, treating the wound a few minutes later, laughed shortly. "Communication by bite, eh, Gard? Where did you bite her?"

Gard called a luncheon conference around the big table in the workroom. Outside the primary sun was setting.

"They *are* animals," he said ruefully to the men around the table. "We've never seen them communicate or cooperate. I doubt they even have voices. I propose we trap one and make him talk to us in action-language, the way we make rats tell us what they can see and remember."

"How can you make a rat talk?" McPherson asked.

"You teach him triangle means food and square means shock, Ike. When he learns to run to one and away from the other then you and he have a common language of two symbols."

"Ed'll be the food," Minelli said. "They think he's yummy."

"Go crawl under a rock, Pete. This is serious."

"Keep on meddling," Onderdonck said under his breath.

Gard firmed his lips. "What do *you* think, Joe?"

"They must have a nervous system adequate for language," Svirsky said. "The symbol-world is in them, in neural impulse pattern and humoral gradient, far more intricately structured than in any rat. But they lack the Word. I suspect they're like a supersaturated solution lacking a mote to crystallize a world around. But drop a primal symbol into them and they may develop language and verbal thought almost explosively."

"Define a primal symbol," Chalmers demanded.

"I can state one but not define it," Svirsky said. "Space, time and the object. It's triune, each member existing by virtue of the other two. It is the zygote of all language."

"Then it's a *verbal* symbol?"

"Yes. It is the cultural aspect or correlate of an immensely older neural symbol. The ontogeny of human language recapitulates the phylogeny of the vertebrate nervous system. Both make a model of the world, but language can *bind time*. If your enemy has no primal symbol, then your own becomes your most precious secret. I speak in riddles, my brothers."

"You speak in metaphor and analogy. That's more poetry than science," Onderdonck sneered.

"And perhaps more truth than poetry," Chalmers said thinly. "I'll be honest, Gard. I fear your curiosity. Much as I dislike admitting it, I feel that some things are dangerous to know too soon. We need to keep firm hold of our world and wait the proper time."

"Ed, you don't mean to feed 'em that primal symbol?" McPherson asked anxiously.

"No, Ike. I wouldn't know how, anyway."

"You might trigger something, not meaning to or knowing, if you fumble around."

"*Precisely,* Ike!" Chalmers said. "Vote with Webb and me to stop all this."

"You promised me a week, people," Gard pleaded. "Let me have the rest of it."

He won a shaky victory. Onderdonck and Chalmers undertook to bring in the observation units and to dismantle and stow the flyer. Gard, McPherson and Minelli set to work on the cage.

The cage was the standard ten-foot cube of reenforced steel mesh. At one end problem boxes flanked a door with an observation unit above it. Sweating in the dim light of the further sun, the men baited the cage and charged one of the boxes with the small ground melons the Proteans ate avidly.

"I'll set this box for a two-lever problem," Gard said. "See, Ike, he'll have to press them in the right sequence to make a melon roll out. He'll do it by random action first, then get the idea. Then we'll make it tougher, record times and trials and so on. I expect he'll learn fast."

They returned to the ship at Protean sunrise. McPherson fixed a late dinner and they ate it in the workroom watching the cage on the stereo screen. Minelli cleaned up the dishes and turned in, leaving Gard and McPherson alone. An hour later a male Protean entered the cage, showing no alarm when the door closed behind him.

"That son of a gun looks just like me," McPherson complained. "I wish he was green or purple."

"Watch him turn purple once he knows he's trapped."

The Protean ate three melons, fumbled at the sticks

Gard had left in the cage, and shambled through its side. The steel mesh was intact.

"Let's us turn purple," McPherson said. "That ain't possible."

Then it hit them. They stared at each other, speechless, then back at the screen. A female Protean came in view. She approached obliquely and seemed to slide through the mesh. She ate two melons and left, as stupidly unaware as when she came. Gard cursed softly.

"Call Joe, Ike. *Only* Joe. I'll brew some coffee."

The three men sipped coffee and watched a Protean eat the last melon in the cage center. McPherson broke the silence.

"This is more'n I can take, Ed. Let's dump it in their laps back on Earth. This calls for a full expedition."

"No, Ike. They'd never get several hundred people away against the jinx, not even six men another time. We're here on a fluke and it's up to us or never."

"You are the fluke, Ed," Svirsky said. "Here's a suggestion. Wind cable around that cage and send high frequency alternating current through it."

"How could that—"

"A hunch, Ed. I've been wondering whether Proteans might not mix space and time into a world-structure different from our own in their neural model of reality. But so does AC mix them in a way strange to our neural model. Try it, Ed."

"Let's do it, Ike."

Gard carried the heavy power pack, McPherson the cable and oscillator. They wound four turns around the cage, looping it over the door. Gard baited the cage with melons from the puzzle box and reset the door. Proteans shambled aimlessly near the cage when the Earthmen walked back sweating under the bright sun. When they entered the workroom the stereo showed a large male already trapped.

He ate the two bait melons leisurely, then walked to the side of the cage and recoiled. The three men watched

as he tried again and again in what seemed a mounting
excitement. He began howling and other Proteans answered and drifted toward the cage, only to recoil from its
outside. They milled in a ragged circle, howling too.

"Well, they do have voices," Gard commented.

"Your hunch paid off, Joe," McPherson said. "We've
got 'em by the tail now."

Svirsky grunted. "So we have, Ike."

It was just midnight, ship-time. By Protean sunset two
hours later the captive became quiet in the cage center
and those outside went away. McPherson and Svirsky
turned in. Gard watched and thought.

Minelli came in just after six. Gard asked him to take
the watch until Protean sunrise at nine. He said nothing
about the earlier escapes.

"I expect Lord Proteus will stay quiet until sunrise.
Then he'll stir and be hungry and tell us how smart he is
through that problem box," he told Minelli.

Gard's sleep was troubled with dreams. He woke to
Minelli's shaking and thought it was still a dream when
the geologist said curtly, "Your man talked, Ed. He said
'Open sesame.'"

"You don't mean he got away?"

"You better come." Minelli left.

All hands were standing before the stereo screen and
all but Svirsky looked at Gard with narrowed eyes, then
back to the screen in silence. Gard saw with relief that his
Protean was still a captive, squatting and shuffling the
sticks. Then, as he watched, a melon dropped through the
side of the problem box. The Protean reached for it,
began eating. The dispensing counter on the box registered zero.

"He does it by random action. *Real* random," Pete Minelli said. He did not smile.

"This does it, you fool," Onderdonck said thickly.
"*Now* we'll vote."

"Ed, agree to lift out right now," McPherson pleaded.

Gard declined. McPherson and Minelli voted with Onderdonck. The fat man, flushed with triumph, looked at Chalmers.

"I don't know, Webb," the biochemist said slowly. "It was bumping against something like this I was hoping to avoid, I think. But now maybe none of us are *fit* to go back to earth."

"We can regain sanity," Onderdonck urged. "Something shielded us from this until that brainsick fool—"

"We've got to make a token fight, now," Chalmers interrupted. "I've *seen* it happen. Each in his own way, perhaps, we must make our fight here, get our teeth into this thing."

"Gard, I feel almost a duty to *kill* you!" Onderdonck cried. "You loosen the bonds of Creation itself, you fool, you fool!" He looked apoplectic.

"Give me the rest of the ship-day," Gard said. "I'm scared too, Onderdonck. We'll lift out by six."

Onderdonck and Minelli left the workroom. The four others watched the Protean repeat his performance seven more times and then rest, apparently sated. Gard and Chalmers cut the record-tape into the nine sequences and fed them through the pattern analyzer, first in parallel and then singly for correlation. The highest reading was point sixteen.

"That's more random than pure chance," Chalmers said. "That may give us a handhold."

"No human action can be *purely* random," Svirsky agreed. "Causality is structured very basically into our wiring diagram, perhaps as far back as the Permian. We can't even perceive pure randomness in our world."

They talked around the subject. "I want to help," McPherson said finally, "but I can't make out how we're going to come to grips with this business. What's the Protean wiring diagram like?"

"I have a notion, from work on lower life-forms," Svirsky said. "I should dissect that fellow in the cage."

"No," Chalmers said. "He's para-human, at the least. How about depth photos?"

Svirsky agreed that might do. They decided to anesthetize the Protean, make depth photos for analysis on Earth, and lift out. Chalmers thought neuralin might not work well in Protean biochemistry and said he would persuade Onderdonck and Minelli to come along and help if restraint were needed. It was one o'clock, ship-time.

"If neuralin works too well, they can help carry back the body," he said. "I wouldn't object to taking a *dead* Protean back to Earth."

Onderdonck and Minelli carried pistols to the cage. Gard went in alone with the neuralin gun. The red-bearded Protean moved to one side, not looking at Gard, and suddenly ran for the door. Gard flung out his powerful left arm and the Protean ran through it.

The men at the door jumped aside. Onderdonck aimed his pistol and Svirsky struck it up. Gard came out, pale and shuddering.

"I can't describe it," he said. "Like being violated in a secret place I couldn't know existed. God! My flesh crawls! I'll go home now, Onderdonck."

"Too late," Onderdonck said, pointing his pistol.

They saw a file of naked Proteans emerging from shrubbery between them and the ship, cutting them off, bearing down obliquely. Minelli cursed and drew his pistol.

"Not yet, Pete," Svirsky said gently. "Into the cage, my brothers."

Inside the closed cage they watched the Proteans, led by a huge, red-bearded male, circle them on a ten-yard radius. When the leader cut through the incoming file to close the circle the Proteans set up an uncadenced howling.

The leader led the file through itself and into a second circle of greater radius. Women and half-grown children spaced randomly with men kept coming in on the long secant. They stepped high and deliberately, arms hanging, howling from expressionless faces. The leader drew a

third loop and then a fourth that lost itself in far trees and hollows. Still they came in on the long slant.

Gard climbed the cage wall to look over their heads. "It looks like a logarithmic spiral," he shouted down. Onderdonck cursed steadily. Svirsky and Chalmers talked into each other's ear against the howling.

After nearly an hour the incoming file ended. The spiral unwound out of sight and the howling died away. The men left the cage.

Minelli laughed uncertainly. "Well, that didn't hurt much," he said.

"God, things seem still and silent after that war dance," McPherson said. "Let's go home, men."

He led off, the others at his heels. After a few steps Chalmers cried "Stop!"

"Things don't look right," he said. "See those trees ahead."

"Blurry and jumping a little," Gard agreed. "Easy now."

"Twisting in circles," McPherson murmured. "It's scary."

"Danger," Chalmers said quietly. "Back by the cage."

From the cage everything looked all right again. It was Protean midafternoon, with a few cumulus clouds overhead. No breeze stirred the gray-green leaves, no birds flew.

"What kind of danger, Hank?" Gard asked.

"Ignorance is danger now. All we know yet is that some influence unstructures our perception, makes the world look like an impressionist painting."

"Monet sweated to *achieve* that vision. Where's the danger?"

"Van Gogh had that vision thrust upon him," Chalmers said crisply, "and it ended by killing him. Let's map out the boundary and mark it with twigs. We'll be our own instruments."

The boundary was a rough circle. The men looked at Gard.

"Now what, Hank?" McPherson asked Chalmers.

"We need more data," Gard said. "Have to know how bad it gets. Maybe it's a belt that lets up again. I'll go out alone, a little further. You watch me, but don't come after me *whatever happens*."

He walked into the zone like a boxer into the ring, his symmetrical athlete's torso gleaming in the sun.

Gard screamed and threshed as they dragged him in by the cage.

"Come out of it, Ed!" Chalmers barked, slapping him. "You're all right."

Gard sat up and shook his head. The others bent above him.

"You wandered like a tapeless robot out there," McPherson said. "When you stumbled back in you flopped and screamed. What happened?"

"First the blur and the vibration of visual things," Gard said slowly. "Then everything came alive and the sky was a big face and I couldn't bear it any more and then *snap*—the dream."

"What did you dream?" Chalmers asked.

"A true thing, Hank, out of my past. When I was ten I fell from a concrete bomb ruin. Part way down rusty rods caught me under the left arm pit and shoulder blade, tore up the brachial plexus—that's how I got this lopsided look and the gimp arm. I hung there—Christ it was awful, living that again!"

He stroked his withered left arm with a wry smile, then stood up.

"Well," Chalmers said. "Disintegration of the world-gestalt. Sudden hypermnesic regression to an earlier personality configuration at a point of trauma. No physical harm, but the subject is incapacitated for rational behavior in present time. I generalize from one instance, as I shouldn't. Words are comforting, but these are only whats. Who'll offer a how?"

"I'll try," Svirsky said. "The Proteans may have a kind of action-space inconceivable to us and probably not conceptual with them. They have thrown a *barrier* around this island of our own action-space—"

"Blank nonsense!" Onderdonck broke in. "Gard is a brainsick fool, that's what and how both. He'll take Webb Onderdonck no further!"

The fat man held a stick from the cage and he shook it toward the ship.

"I can *see* the ship," he said. "This is some kind of optical razzle-dazzle, but where this stick can go Webb Onderdonck can follow. I'll *close* my damned eyes!"

He strode off, jabbing the stick angrily into the ground ahead of him with each step.

"There walks a man braver than he is able to know," Svirsky said softly.

They drew together and watched him go, stick jabbing, undeviating, and *tension rose and gripped them in a great collective shudder.*

"Their action-space overpowers our own, limits us and frees us in ways inconceivable."

"But how? There's danger, God knows we all five feel it now, but let's put a finger on it," Chalmers said.

"Death, maybe," Gard said. "When I fell, I caught a ledge with my fingers. It seemed to me I deliberately let go. When I hung on those rods I screamed as much in frustration as in pain."

"So?"

"So maybe the thing that says 'I' can't bear disintegration of the symbol system. Maybe it *is* the symbol system, something emergent at a high level of abstraction and integration, oh dammit, something modulated onto the body's life like information on a carrier wave, a thing of words only—don't mind me, people. I'm talking in tongues."

"Hardly a revelation. But go on."

"All right, in desperation out there we might become

able to flash back along ourselves to a point of danger and tip the scales for death. I tell you, I *felt* it!"

"The pain I grant you, but not the danger. Suppose you *had* killed yourself, aged ten. Then you couldn't have made that unauthorized tape-substitution and we wouldn't be here. But we are here."

"Someone else would have done it, perhaps you."

"That's changing the *past*," McPherson said angrily.

"The past would be intact all the way back to Creation, for all you could ever determine," Gard said. "But I'd be dead."

"I just can't *think* it, Ed."

"None of us can think it in our bones and muscles, Ike," Svirsky said, "but we can still talk about it in words. Listen now, not with your muscles. Each of us is a world-line in a four-dimensional continuum that contains a certain *irreversibility*. To know ourselves, we segregate the irreversibility into one dimension and call it time. Then we experience ourselves as free in the other three dimensions. Suppose now, not with your muscles, that the Proteans handle the irreversibility differently. They have made a cage for us, as we for them, but of their own world-stuff."

"Show me a crucial test for that hypothesis and I'll buy it, Joe," Chalmers said. "But you do give me an idea. We have long known how language both structures and reflects the structure of the microcosm which we project into the world and what a *social* process it is. We may be able to overcome this disintegrating influence by going out in company and *talking* constantly."

"Not all of us," Gard said sharply. "We might all flash back and get hurt or die and this trip would never have been. I won't have that."

"You mean to coerce history by holding back a hostage? I talk in words, I talk in words!"

"Yes. There may also be a least action factor that makes prevention of suicide more probable than bodily replacement."

"I wish we *could* cancel this trip!" Minelli burst out. "That guy Onderdonck that broke his back ski-jumping just before we left must've known what he was doing. God knows how *we'll* end."

"I see your point, Ed, but I prefer to call it a control. Whom shall we leave?"

"Joe and yourself," McPherson said. "In time you two will hammer this thing out flat, I feel it. We can't risk you."

Chalmers demurred and was shouted down. Gard's right hand clasped McPherson's left strongly. Minelli had firm hold of Gard's left wrist. The three men moved out, talking steadily.

Look, the tree's blurry. Pete, Pete, pick out the leaves. Keep seeing the leaves, well the branches then don't let it get solid pull off a twig man feel it bite it bleeding the tree screamed bending at me the earth the grass pull it bleed ingand foldingover God'seyeupthen . . .

". . . eat mud, Ed Gard. You said it's no different up here than on the ground."

"Must be a hundred-foot drop."

"So the I-beam is still just as wide as the one you walked down below. With your eyes closed, down below. Eat mud, Ed Gard."

"I'm scared. But I won't eat mud."

"Eat mud, Ed Gard." .

"Here goes, damn you. Just as wide, nothing to it . . ."

. . . *armsthrashingco lorsflashing the fear the fear jerking him along past lump trees a man too, and there Svirsky reaching out, the zone, of course, clearing now, all right now.*

Mary Gard let go of Vane's hand and looked ruefully at Chalmers.

"Well, Hank, talking doesn't help," she said.

"That's data too, Mary. What did you experience, Chuck? Time suicide?"

"Hell no," Vane said. "We talked and things went hor-

rible anyway and then bang, we were still talking, but it was back in my office in Denver. A real memory-dream, like. Mary was just telling me about Ike McPherson being arrested for rape and it was an hour before lift out. She was crying."

"Can you really cry, Mary?" Chalmers asked.

"Tears of rage, Hank," Mary said. "I couldn't bear being thwarted. Even with only Chuck and I knowing the secret, the jinx still worked. Onderdonck broke his back and Minelli got cut up in a tavern brawl and that was all right, we could go short-handed. But we *had* to have a shipman."

"She knew I was licensed," Vane took up the story. "She said it was Earth's last chance to solve the mystery of Proteus and she *wouldn't* let it go, was I a man or a mouse, and me saying I'd be busted out of the Corps and my wife screaming mad and both of us still saying it as she dragged me up the gangplank."

"That doesn't support your death-urge hypothesis, Mary," Chalmers said.

"Mine does again. Maybe it's just me," Mary said. "I went back to an experience of my father's, a bad fall that kept him out of school for a year. It was eerie—death waiting and a kind of voluptuous *wanting* to fall. I could *feel* myself taunting myself into it, swinging myself into vertigo, yet it was my father all the time."

"But your father survived. Even granting that your consciousness can cross a world-line synapse into a parent, you haven't changed anything. Chuck's experience was innocuous. Our solid evidence indicates only loss of awareness and coordination in present time."

"Even so, that's dangerous," Vane said. "We couldn't man the ship in that state. The wolf-things or even the Proteans could eat us alive."

"Chuck, that's the how!" Mary cried. "Remember how the Proteans seem to paralyze or uncoordinate the goat-things they sometimes eat? I'll bet they just *run around them*. Remember how they walked around us and we felt angry and had headaches and how I conked out and got bitten on my bad arm? They were trying to put us in cages then and we were too strong. So now they've done it massively. It's as if we'd made our cage out of armor plate after the first one failed."

"That's part of the what, not the how," Chalmers objected, "and your argument is from analogy—"

"Which may be perfectly good *Protean* logic," Svirsky interrupted. "It's a Protean cage we're in. No how will satisfy you until we reduce it to touch and kinesthesis. But this how is different. Consider, our bodies are not caged but our minds are."

"How can a *mind* be *caged?*" Vane asked.

"When we know, we will escape," Svirsky said. "We must play a word game now apart from muscle-thinking. We are in a time trap. Here in our cage our entropy increases. I am thirsty. I feel the heat of that sun, but I marked the cage shadow after our first alarm and in all our scramblings since *that sun has not moved.*"

Chalmers paled. "That's something I can grasp, anyway. It supports Mary's weird notion about changing the past. That stillness out there. Time stasis. To be conscious is to be conscious of *change* . . . now I talk in tongues, Mary."

"It's only a word game, Hank. Keep talking."

"All right, changing the past, words only," Vane said. "Coercing history by leaving someone behind. That dream I had out there, damn it, I *wanted* to tell Mary to go to hell and I couldn't. Maybe that was history coercing me. But let's all go out now, and if I hit that sequence again you can damn well bet I'll refuse and we'll be out of this fix. Word game!"

"No," Mary said. "I won't have it so."

"We can't really change the past, Mary, and you know it," Chalmers said. "Both times you were out you trended to the left under a kind of tropism that brought you back in. The worst that can happen is that we will all have a shaking up and a bad dream. But how do we know that this *island* of ours will not move with us if we all go? We must use trial and error until we have enough data for an operational hypothesis."

"Muscle-thinking," Svirsky said. "But let's try it, Hank. We can pick up our word game afterward."

"I'm coming back," Mary warned.

Svirsky's big hand encircled her left wrist.

Water black as the night sky above swirled around Thomas Gard's chest. His small son in the crook of his left arm whimpered into his ear. His wife was losing her footing, clinging to his right elbow, pulling him over.

"Climb up on me, Mary," he said, stooping a little. "Let me carry you both. We'll be swept away else."

"You haven't the strength, Tom. Let me go, save Edward."

"All of us or none of us, Mary. Only a hundred yards now."

"Too far. I know it. Edward, goodbye Edward, you be a brave, strong man now."

"Mary!"

"Goodbye, Tom. I love you."

The current swept her into darkness. Thomas Gard

shouted her name in anguish over the black, swirling water. The child cried in a greater fear.

The four men stumbled into present awareness by the metal cage, still holding hands. Chalmers was trembling.

"I grant you that death-urge now, Ed," he gasped, "but don't ask me——"

"Never mind, Hank," Gard said. "Let's be convinced now that charging bullheaded into it isn't going to change a thing. We have to *think* our minds free of this."

"God yes," McPherson said. "I relived that fight I had with Vane when he tried to restrict me to the base the night before liftout. I felt *murderous,* I tell you. He kept getting up and I beat him almost to death. I thought I'd get a year in jail."

"He was trying to beat the jinx on Proteus," Gard said. "That's why he restricted you and also why he wouldn't bring charges."

"The fight bothered me," McPherson admitted. "I went on to the party, but I couldn't get drunk. I didn't have enough steam and ugliness left in me to carry through that near-rape I relived the first time out. Funny how things hang together."

"Isn't it, though? I went through a crucial episode in my grandfather's life, a flood. I was three people and this time I think I accepted death while willing life. But that's not data, even for a word game."

"I'll play now, Joe," Chalmers said. "Start your word game."

"Let your muscles hear this part," Svirsky said. "Sit down and relax."

They sprawled on the dull green grass.

"We vertebrates define time, space and thingness first in our own bodies," Svirsky began. "Then we generalize them to all sensory input to make a real world. It was an action-world for a billion years before it became a thought-world, and it is muscles which act. Our wiring diagram provides our muscles with two separate innervation circuits.

"One circuit is for muscle tone and it never relaxes completely until death. It maintains posture, any unchanging position we hold through time. It does it by continuous motor discharge from and kinesthetic sensory feedback to the cerebellum. From the cerebellum association fibers go to the cerebral cortex and almost all of this innervation is on the *same* side of the body as the muscles concerned.

"Suppose for the moment that tonus underlies our basic feeling of time as duration.

"The phasic innervation provides for action, the causing of relative position changes among things. It starts from the motor area of the cortex and feeds back to an adjacent sensory area. Both areas on both hemispheres have the shapes of grotesque manikins. Discriminatory touch, pain and temperature also feed into the sensory areas. But the fibers nearly all *cross over* from muscles and skin on the *opposite* side of the body.

"Suppose now that phasis underlies our root-feeling for space and change. Suppose further that its cortical projection areas are superimposed on the uncrossed sensory-tonic projection from the cerebellum. Suppose finally that combination of sameness-in-difference gives us the stubbornly felt *apartness* of time from space and, in the tension between them, thingness. Number, magnitude, causality, the world, can follow.

"We know our language structures our thought and the world we experience. But the structure of our nervous system, our coding and uncoding equipment, provides language itself with an invariant pattern upon which linguistic relativity is only secondary elaboration.

"All of this, my brothers, is to persuade your muscles not to listen to what I wish to say next."

Gard flexed his powerful left arm. "You just go along for the ride, now," he addressed his biceps.

"Almost you make me touch the how of how itself," Chalmers mused. "Go on with the word game. My muscles are out of circuit."

Svirsky smiled. "The Protean vertebrate wiring diagram," he said, "does not provide for tract crossings in the cord. The brain is imperfectly divided and has no bundled commissures. Like us, they code the world in volleys of neural impulse, but their decoding equipment is *different*.

"Like us, they exist in the continuum as world-lines. They have wound around our own thin sheaf of world-lines a massive coil of their world-lines. It makes a time cage that coerces our world-lines in a way our muscles cannot *grasp*."

"You mean they outvoted us muscleheads?" McPherson asked.

"They have more of their kind of muscle, Ike," Chalmers agreed. "But Joe, do you mean we have to grasp *their* reality?"

"We must stop trying to *grasp* it. I said our vertebrate wiring diagram may dictate our primal symbol of reality. But some few of the fibers in each case I cited do not follow the structural rule. And we have also, below consciousness, a phylogenetically older diagram. These are ghosts within us, my brothers, not bound to the primal symbol. Let us wake them now.

"Let go of lever and pushrod causality for the notion of statistical covariance. Let go of that for the still more primitive notion of 'organism' and 'sympathy of the

whole' out of which both arise. Remember that fairly late
in the pre-space era our own ancestors used to bewitch
each other and one potent how was to run nine times
widdershins around the victim. Think of that timeless,
spaceless, pre-vertebral 'sympathy of the whole' as the
substrate from which parapsychological phenomena still
arise to bedevil science centuries after Rhine."

"You mean we're bewitched, then?" Chalmers asked.

"That's the simplest how that we can dredge out of our
symbol system," Svirsky agreed. "We are under a spell so
powerful that our massed rationality cannot prevail
against it at any cost. So we must erect your operational
hypothesis on an irrational base.

"Here is one. We are caged by a field effect. When we
cut across it consciousness drops almost to a cellular level
and the coordinating 'I' flees screaming. But fields have
structure. We must find a geodesic and it may lead us
out."

"We can only grasp fields instrumentally," Chalmers
objected. "But of course, *we* can be the instruments. To
hell with observer detachment."

"Exactly," Svirsky smiled. "Each time Ed trended to
the left out there, I think the pre-vertebral ghost in him
was seeking the geodesic."

"I'll be the instrument," Gard said. "How do you cali-
brate me?"

"You're already calibrated, in degrees of rationality on
scales of perception and speech," Svirsky said. "Get me
two of those sticks you meant to use in playing Kohler to
the Proteans."

He took out his shoelaces and tied an eight-foot stick
to each of Gard's upper arms.

"So I steer you, Ed, when the pointer swings off optimum," he said. "See, we play Kohler to ourselves now."

Gard slanted leftward into the critical area. "The mus-
clehead leading the muscleheads," he laughed. "Here we
go, people."

He described what he saw and Svirsky held him to

coherence with tugs and nudges. Very shortly Gard learned to correct for himself. He followed an erratic, looping, doubling course that still trended leftward. After the first lap around the cage Chalmers remarked that it was a spiral of opposite hand to the Protean mass-spiral.

"That's our statistical trend," Svirsky chuckled, "but who will write the equation for the path we actually follow?"

"We really must work up the statistical dynamics of witchcraft someday," Chalmers laughed back. "Teach every sophomore how to unrun a spell."

The fifth lap missed the ship's ramp by twenty feet. McPherson was dismayed, but Chalmers laughed again.

"I always knew Finagle was a Protean," he said. "We forgot to add his constant to the right hand vector."

"We'll add it now," Svirsky said. "Ed, untie the sticks. Now imagine yourself running to the top of that ramp. Flex your muscles for each step. Experience yourself at the top looking down. Then pull the trigger and *make it so*. Can you do that?"

"Sure," Gard said.

He looked up and down the ramp, pranced a little, then dashed to the top through a blur of motion. He turned, only to be knocked flat by three hurtling bodies.

"Take it *easy*," Gard said, getting up. "It's good to be home, but not *that* good, people."

"We stood down there at least five minutes deciding why you were frozen like a statue up here," Chalmers said. "Then Ike came up and froze, then Joe, and finally I came. We all got here at the exact, same instant."

"I see. We snapped back into our own time. But Joe, how could you know we'd be out of the field up here? Is it a ship effect?"

"Another hunch, Ed. I suspected the Proteans might only project space in two directions so that the field might attenuate rapidly on the vertical."

"Well what d'ye know!" McPherson said disgustedly.

"We could just as well have walked out on stilts. So damned *simple*! How stupid can you get?"

"Science can't answer that question," Chalmers said.

"Stations," Gard said. "Let's lift out, Ike."

In subspace, on automatics, the four of them relaxed with coffee.

"Our report," Gard said. "I propose we rig it and conclude that Proteus is not only unsuitable for settlement but of no interest to commerce, science or even art."

"Right," Chalmers agreed. "How could we ever *tell* them otherwise?"

"Oh, I don't know," McPherson said. "Use Joe's line about fields. People savvy fields, all right."

"Yes," Chalmers said. "Fences around them. Flowers and grass. When a man's in a field he's got both feet on the ground."

"Joe," Gard broke in, "I think you knew more all along than you let on. Why didn't you come up with that explanation sooner? Of course nobody got hurt, but you did let us all bloody our noses on that barrier."

"Maybe I could have, Ed," Svirsky admitted. "Maybe I even wanted to. But if I had, my brothers, it would have seemed to all of us too silly for words."

"Not to speak of action," Chalmers said softly.

If Joanna Russ had consulted me before beginning to write her Alyx stories (see "I Gave Her Sack and Sherry" and "The Adventuress," in Orbit 2*), I would have told her nobody could get away with a series of heroic fantasies of prehistory in which the central character, the barbaric adventurer, is a woman. I would have been wrong, just as I was when I told Rosel George Brown she couldn't sell a novel about a female private eye. [See* Sibyl Sue Blue, *Doubleday, 1966; Berkley, 1967 (published as* Galactic Sibyl Sue Blue*).]*

It is a little idiotic, isn't it, that women in adventure stories should have been restricted to the roles of simpering princesses and insatiable vampires? . . . and that even women writers, crushed by convention, should have been too timid to tell us what women are really like?

The attractive thing about Alyx is that she is not a cardboard fantasy figure, but a real person. And incidentally, this is the overlooked clue to the age-old "mystery" about women: they are people.

The Barbarian

by Joanna Russ

Alyx, the gray-eyed, the silent woman. Wit, arm, kill-
quick for hire, she watched the strange man thread his
way through the tables and the smoke toward her. This
was in Ourdh, where all things are possible. He stopped
at the table where she sat alone and with a certain
indefinable gallantry, not pleasant but perhaps its exact
opposite, he said:

"A woman—here?"

"You're looking at one," said Alyx dryly, for she did
not like his tone. It occurred to her that she had seen him
before—though he was not so fat then, no, not quite so
fat—and then it occurred to her that the time of their last
meeting had almost certainly been in the hills when she
was four or five years old. That was thirty years ago. So
she watched him very narrowly as he eased himself into
the seat opposite, watched him as he drummed his fingers
in a lively tune on the tabletop, and paid him close attention when he tapped one of the marine decorations that
hung from the ceiling (a stuffed blowfish, all spikes and
parchment, that moved lazily to and fro in a wandering
current of air) and made it bob. He smiled, the flesh
around his eyes straining into folds.

"I know you," he said. "A raw country girl fresh from
the hills who betrayed an entire religious delegation to the
police some ten years ago. You settled down as a picklock. You made a good thing of it. You expanded your

profession to include a few more difficult items and you did a few things that turned heads hereabouts. You were not unknown, even then. Then you vanished for a season and reappeared as a fairly rich woman. But that didn't last, unfortunately."

"Didn't have to," said Alyx.

"Didn't last," repeated the fat man imperturbably, with a lazy shake of the head. "No, no, it didn't last. And now," (he pronounced the "now" with peculiar relish) "you are getting old."

"Old enough," said Alyx, amused.

"Old," said he, "old. Still neat, still tough, still small. But old. You're thinking of settling down."

"Not exactly."

"Children?"

She shrugged, retiring a little into the shadow. The fat man did not appear to notice.

"It's been done," she said.

"You may die in childbirth," said he, "at your age."

"That, too, has been done."

She stirred a little, and in a moment a short-handled Southern dagger, the kind carried unobtrusively in sleeves or shoes, appeared with its point buried in the tabletop, vibrating ever so gently.

"It is true," said she, "that I am growing old. My hair is threaded with white. I am developing a chunky look around the waist that does not exactly please me, though I was never a ballet-girl." She grinned at him in the semi-darkness. "Another thing," she said softly, "that I develop with age is a certain lack of patience. If you do not stop making personal remarks and taking up my time—which is valuable—I shall throw you across the room."

"I would not, if I were you," he said.

"You could not."

The fat man began to heave with laughter. He heaved until he choked. Then he said, gasping, "I beg your pardon." Tears ran down his face.

"Go on," said Alyx. He leaned across the table, smiling, his fingers mated tip to tip, his eyes little pits of shadow in his face.

"I come to make you rich," he said.

"You can do more than that," said she steadily. A quarrel broke out across the room between a soldier and a girl he had picked up for the night; the fat man talked through it, or rather under it, never taking his eyes off her face.

"Ah!" he said, "you remember when you saw me last and you assume that a man who can live thirty years without growing older must have more to give—if he wishes—than a handful of gold coins. You are right. I can make you live long. I can insure your happiness. I can determine the sex of your children. I can cure all diseases. I can even" (and here he lowered his voice) "turn this table, or this building, or this whole city to pure gold, if I wish it."

"Can anyone do that?" said Alyx, with the faintest whisper of mockery.

"I can," he said. "Come outside and let us talk. Let me show you a few of the things I can do. I have some business here in the city that I must attend to myself and I need a guide and an assistant. That will be you."

"If you can turn the city into gold," said Alyx just as softly, "can you turn gold into a city?"

"Anyone can do that," he said, laughing; "come along," so they rose and made their way into the cold outside air—it was a clear night in early spring—and at a corner of the street where the moon shone down on the walls and the pits in the road, they stopped.

"Watch," said he.

On his outstretched palm was a small black box. He shook it, turning it this way and that, but it remained wholly featureless. Then he held it out to her and, as she took it in her hand, it began to glow until it became like a piece of glass lit up from the inside. There in the middle of it was her man, with his tough, friendly, young-old face and his hair a little gray, like hers. He smiled at her, his lips moving soundlessly. She threw the cube into the air a few times, held it to the side of her face, shook it, and then dropped it on the ground, grinding it under her heel. It remained unhurt.

She picked it up and held it out to him, thinking:

Not metal, very light. And warm. A toy? Wouldn't break, though. Must be some sort of small machine, though God knows who made it and of what. It follows thoughts! Marvelous. But magic? Bah! Never believed in it before; why now? Besides, this thing too sensible; magic is elaborate, undependable, useless. I'll tell him—but then it occurred to her that someone had gone to a good deal of trouble to impress her when a little bit of credit might have done just as well. And this man walked with an almighty confidence through the streets for someone who was unarmed. And those thirty years—so she said very politely:

"It's magic!"

He chuckled and pocketed the cube.

"You're a little savage," he said, "but your examination of it was most logical. I like you. Look! I am an old magician. There is a spirit in that box and there are more spirits under my control than you can possibly imagine. I am like a man living among monkeys. There are things spirits cannot do—or things I choose to do myself, take it any way you will. So I pick one of the monkeys who seems brighter than the rest and train it. I pick you. What do you say?"

"All right," said Alyx.

"Calm enough!" he chuckled. "Calm enough! Good. What's your motive?"

"Curiosity," said Alyx. "It's a monkeylike trait." He chuckled again; his flesh choked it and the noise came out in a high, muffled scream.

"And what if I bite you," said Alyx, "like a monkey?"

"No, little one," he answered gaily, "you won't. You may be sure of that." He held out his hand, still shaking with mirth. In the palm lay a kind of blunt knife which he pointed at one of the whitewashed walls that lined the street. The edges of the wall burst into silent smoke, the whole section trembled and slid, and in an instant it had vanished, vanished as completely as if it had never existed, except for a sullen glow at the raw edges of brick and a pervasive smell of burning. Alyx swallowed.

"It's quiet, for magic," she said softly. "Have you ever used it on men?"

"On armies, little one."

So the monkey went to work for him. There seemed as yet to be no harm in it. The little streets admired his generosity and the big ones his good humor; while those too high for money or flattery he won by a catholic ability that was—so the little picklock thought—remarkable in one so stupid. For about his stupidity there could be no doubt. She smelled it. It offended her. It made her twitch in her sleep, like a ferret. There was in this woman—well hidden away—an anomalous streak of quiet humanity that abhorred him, that set her teeth on edge at the thought of him, though she could not have put into words just what was the matter. *For stupidity,* she thought, *is hardly—is not exactly—*

Four months later they broke into the governor's villa. She thought she might at last find out what this man was after besides pleasure jaunts around the town. Moreover, breaking and entering always gave her the keenest pleasure; and doing so "for nothing" (as he said) tickled her fancy immensely. The power in gold and silver that attracts thieves was banal, in this thief's opinion, but to stand in the shadows of a sleeping house, absolutely silent, with no object at all in view and with the knowledge that if you are found you will probably have your throat cut—! She began to think better of him. This dilettante passion for the craft, this reckless silliness seemed to her as worthy as the love of a piece of magnetite for the North and South poles—the "faithful stone" they call it in Ourdh.

"Who'll come with us?" she asked, wondering for the fiftieth time where the devil he went when he was not with her, whom he knew, where he lived, and what that persistently bland expression on his face could possibly mean.

"No one," he said calmly.

"What are we looking for?"

"Nothing."

"Do you ever do anything for a reason?"

"Never." And he chuckled.

And then, "Why are you so fat?" demanded Alyx, halfway out of her own door, half into the shadows. She had recently settled in a poor quarter of the town, partly out of laziness, partly out of necessity. The shadows playing in the hollows of her face, the expression of her eyes veiled, she said it again, "Why are you so goddamned fat!" He laughed until he wheezed.

"The barbarian mind!" he cried, lumbering after her in high good humor, "Oh—oh, my dear!—oh, what freshness!" She thought:

That's it! and then

The fool doesn't even know I hate him.

But neither had she known, until that very moment.

They scaled the northeast garden wall of the villa and crept along the top of it without descending, for the governor kept dogs. Alyx, who could walk a taut rope like a circus performer, went quietly. The fat man giggled. She swung herself up to the nearest window and hung there by one arm and a toehold for fifteen mortal minutes while she sawed through the metal hinge of the shutter with a file. Once inside the building (he had to be pulled through the window) she took him by the collar with uncanny accuracy, considering that the inside of the villa was stone dark. "Shut up!" she said, with considerable emphasis.

"Oh?" he whispered.

"I'm in charge here," she said, releasing him with a

jerk, and melted into the blackness not two feet away, moving swiftly along the corridor wall. Her fingers brushed lightly alongside her, like a creeping animal: stone, stone, a gap, warm air rising . . . In the dark she felt wolfish, her lips skinned back over her teeth; like another species she made her way with hands and ears. Through them the villa sighed and rustled in its sleep. She put the tips of the fingers of her free hand on the back of the fat man's neck, guiding him with the faintest of touches through the turns of the corridor. They crossed an empty space where two halls met; they retreated noiselessly into a room where a sleeper lay breathing against a dimly lit window, while someone passed in the corridor outside. When the steps faltered for a moment, the fat man gasped and Alyx wrung his wrist, hard. There was a cough from the corridor, the sleeper in the room stirred and murmured, and the steps passed on. They crept back to the hall. Then he told her where he wanted to go.

"What!" She had pulled away, astonished, with a reckless hiss of indrawn breath. Methodically he began poking her in the side and giving her little pushes with his other hand—she moving away, outraged—but all in silence. In the distant reaches of the building something fell—or someone spoke—and without thinking, they waited silently until the sounds had faded away. He resumed his continual prodding. Alyx, her teeth on edge, began to creep forward, passing a cat that sat outlined in the vague light from a window, perfectly unconcerned with them and rubbing its paws against its face, past a door whose cracks shone yellow, past ghostly staircases that opened up in vast wells of darkness, breathing a faint, far updraft, their steps rustling and creaking. They were approaching the governor's nursery. The fat man watched without any visible horror—or any interest, for that matter—while Alyx disarmed the first guard, stalking him as if he were a sparrow, then the one strong pressure on the blood vessel at the back of the neck (all with no noise except the man's own breathing; she was quiet as a shadow). Now he was trussed up, conscious and glaring, quite unable to move. The second guard was asleep in his chair. The third Alyx decoyed out the anteroom by a thrown pebble (she had picked up several in the street). She was three motionless feet away from him as he stooped to examine it; he never straightened up. The fourth guard (he was in the anteroom, in a feeble glow that stole through the hangings of the nursery beyond) turned to greet his friend—or so he thought—and then Alyx judged she could risk a little speech. She said thoughtfully, in a low voice, "That's dangerous, on the back of the head."

"Don't let it bother you," said the fat man. Through the parting of the hangings they could see the nurse, asleep on her couch with her arms bare and their golden circlets gleaming in the lamplight, the black slave in a profound huddle of darkness at the farther door, and a shining, tented basket—the royal baby's royal house. The baby was asleep. Alyx stepped inside—motioning the fat man away from the lamp—and picked the governor's daughter out of her gilt cradle. She went round the apartment with the baby in one arm, bolting both doors and closing the hangings, draping the fat man in a guard's cloak and turning down the lamp so that a bare glimmer of light reached the farthest walls.

"Now you've seen it," she said, "shall we go?"

He shook his head. He was watching her curiously, his head tilted to one side. He smiled at her. The baby woke up and began to chuckle at finding herself carried about; she grabbed at Alyx's mouth and jumped up and down, bending in the middle like a sort of pocket-compass or enthusiastic spring. The woman lifted her head to avoid the baby's fingers and began to soothe her, rocking her in her arms. "Good Lord, she's cross-eyed," said Alyx. The nurse and her slave slept on, wrapped in the profoundest unconsciousness. Humming a little, soft tune to the governor's daughter, Alyx walked her about the room, humming and rocking, rocking and humming, until the baby yawned.

"Better go," said Alyx.

"No," said the fat man.

"Better," said Alyx again. "One cry and the nurse—"

"Kill the nurse," said the fat man.

"The slave—"

"He's dead." Alyx started, rousing the baby. The slave still slept by the door, blacker than the blackness, but under him oozed something darker still in the twilight flame of the lamp. "You did that?" whispered Alyx, hushed. She had not seen him move. He took something dark and hollow, like the shell of a nut, from the palm of his hand and laid it next the baby's cradle; with a shiver half of awe and half of distaste Alyx put that richest and most fortunate daughter of Ourdh back into her gilt cradle. Then she said:

"Now we'll go."

"But I have not what I came for," said the fat man.

"And what is that?"

"The baby."

"Do you mean to steal her?" said Alyx curiously.

"No," said he, "I mean for you to kill her."

The woman stared. In sleep the governor's daughter's nurse stirred; then she sat bolt upright, said something incomprehensible in a loud voice, and fell back to her couch, still deep in sleep. So astonished was the picklock that she did not move. She only looked at the fat man. Then she sat by the cradle and rocked it mechanically with one hand while she looked at him.

"What on earth for?" she said at length. He smiled. He seemed as easy as if he were discussing her wages or the price of pigs; he sat down opposite her and he too rocked the cradle, looking on the burden it contained with a benevolent, amused interest. If the nurse had woken up at that moment, she might have thought she saw the governor and his wife, two loving parents who had come to visit their child by lamplight. The fat man said:

"Must you know?"

"I must," said Alyx.

"Then I will tell you," said the fat man, "not because you must, but because I choose. This little six-months morsel is going to grow up."

"Most of us do," said Alyx, still astonished.

"She will become a queen," the fat man went on, "and a surprisingly wicked woman for one who now looks so innocent. She will be the death of more than one child and more than one slave. In plain fact, she will be a horror to the world. This I know."

"I believe you," said Alyx, shaken.

"Then kill her," said the fat man. But still the picklock did not stir. The baby in her cradle snored, as infants sometimes do, as if to prove the fat man's opinion of her by showing a surprising precocity; still the picklock did not move, but stared at the man across the cradle as if he were a novel work of nature.

"I ask you to kill her," said he again.

"In twenty years," said she, "when she has become so very wicked."

"Woman, are you deaf? I told you—"

"In twenty years!" In the feeble light from the lamp she appeared pale, as if with rage or terror. He leaned deliberately across the cradle, closing his hand around the shell or round-shot or unidentifiable object he had dropped there a moment before; he said very deliberately:

"In twenty years you will be dead."

"Then do it yourself," said Alyx softly, pointing at the object in his hand, "unless you had only one?"

"I had only one."

"Ah, well then," she said, "here!" and she held out to him across the sleeping baby the handle of her dagger, for she had divined something about this man in the months they had known each other; and when he made no move to take the blade, she nudged his hand with the handle.

"You don't like things like this, do you?" she said.

"Do as I say, woman!" he whispered. She pushed the handle into his palm. She stood up and poked him deliberately with it, watching him tremble and sweat; she had never seen him so much at a loss. She moved round the cradle, smiling and stretching out her arm seductively. "Do as I say!" he cried.

"Softly, softly."

"You're a sentimental fool!"

"Am I?" she said. "Whatever I do, I must feel; I can't just twiddle my fingers like you, can I?"

"Ape!"

"You chose me for it."

"Do as I say!"

"Sh! You will wake the nurse." For a moment both stood silent, listening to the baby's all-but-soundless breathing and the rustling of the nurse's sheets. Then he said, "Woman, your life is in my hands."

"Is it?" said she.

"I want your obedience!"

"Oh no," she said softly, "I know what you want. You want importance because you have none; you want to swallow up another soul. You want to make me fear you and I think you can succeed, but I think also that I can teach you the difference between fear and respect. Shall I?"

"Take care!" he gasped.

"Why?" she said. "Lest you kill me?"

"There are other ways," he said, and he drew himself up, but here the picklock spat in his face. He let out a strangled wheeze and lurched backwards, stumbling against the curtains. Behind her Alyx heard a faint cry; she whirled about to see the governor's nurse sitting up in bed, her eyes wide open.

"Madam, quietly, quietly," said Alyx, "for God's sake!"

The governor's nurse opened her mouth.

"I have done no harm," said Alyx passionately, "I swear it!" but the governor's nurse took a breath with the

clear intention to scream, a hearty, healthy, full-bodied
scream like the sort picklocks hear in nightmares. In the
second of the governor's nurse's shuddering inhalation—
in that split second that would mean unmentionably unpleasant things for Alyx, as Ourdh was not a kind city—
Alyx considered launching herself at the woman, but the
cradle was between. It would be too late. The house
would be roused in twenty seconds. She could never
make it to a door—or a window—not even to the garden,
where the governor's hounds could drag down a stranger
in two steps. All these thoughts flashed through the picklock's mind as she saw the governor's nurse inhale with
that familiar, hideous violence; her knife was still in her
hand; with the smooth simplicity of habit it slid through
her fingers and sped across the room to bury itself in the
governor's nurse's neck, just above the collarbone in that
tender hollow Ourdhian poets love to sing of. The woman's open-mouthed expression froze on her face; with an
"uh!" of surprise she fell forward, her arms hanging limp
over the edge of the couch. A noise came from her
throat. The knife had opened a major pulse, and in the
blood's slow, powerful, rhythmic tides across sheet and
slippers and floor Alyx could discern a horrid similarity
to the posture and appearance of the black slave. One
was hers, one was the fat man's. She turned and hurried
through the curtains into the anteroom, only noting that
the soldier blindfolded and bound in the corner had managed patiently to work loose the thongs around two of his
fingers with his teeth. He must have been at it all this
time. Outside in the hall the darkness of the house was as
undisturbed as if the nursery were that very Well of
Peace whence the gods first drew (as the saying is) the
dawn and the color—but nothing else—for the eyes of
women. On the wall someone had written in faintly shining stuff, like snail-slime, the single word *Fever*.

But the fat man was gone.

Her man was raving and laughing on the floor when
she got home. She could not control him—she could only

sit with her hands over her face and shudder—so at length she locked him in and gave the key to the old woman who owned the house, saying, "My husband drinks too much. He was perfectly sober when I left earlier this evening and now look at him. Don't let him out."

Then she stood stock-still for a moment, trembling and thinking: of the fat man's distaste for walking, of his wheezing, his breathlessness, of his vanity that surely would have led him to show her any magic vehicle he had that took him to whatever he called home. He must have walked. She had seen him go out the north gate a hundred times.

She began to run.

To the south Ourdh is built above marshes that will engulf anyone or anything unwary enough to try to cross them, but to the north the city peters out into sand dunes fringing the seacoast and a fine monotony of rocky hills that rise to a countryside of sandy scrub, stunted trees and what must surely be the poorest farms in the world. Ourdh believes that these farmers dream incessantly of robbing travelers, so nobody goes there, all the fashionable world frequenting the great north road that loops a good fifty miles to avoid this region. Even without its stories the world would have no reason to go here; there is nothing to see but dunes and weeds and now and then a shack (or more properly speaking, a hut) resting on an outcropping of rock or nesting right on the sand like a toy boat in a basin. There is only one landmark in the whole place—an old tower hardly even fit for a wizard —and that was abandoned nobody knows how long ago, though it is only twenty minutes' walk from the city gates. Thus it was natural that Alyx (as she ran, her heart pounding in her side) did not notice the stars, or the warm night-wind that stirred the leaves of the trees, or indeed the very path under her feet; though she knew all the paths for twenty-five miles around. Her whole mind was on that tower. She felt its stones stick in her throat.

On her right and left the country flew by, but she seemed not to move; at last, panting and trembling, she crept through a nest of tree-trunks no thicker than her wrist (they were very old and very tough) and sure enough, there it was. There was a light shining halfway between bottom and top. Then someone looked out, like a cautious householder out of an attic, and the light went out.

Ah! thought she, and moved into the cover of the trees. The light—which had vanished—now reappeared a story higher and so on, higher and higher, until it reached the top. It wobbled a little, as if held in the hand. So this was his country seat! Silently and with great care, she made her way from one pool of shadow to another. One hundred feet from the tower she circled it and approached it from the northern side. A finger of the sea cut in very close to the base of the building (it had been slowly falling into the water for many years) and in this she first waded and then swam, disturbing the faint, cold radiance of the starlight in the placid ripples. There was no moon. Under the very walls of the tower she stopped and listened; in the darkness under the sea she felt along the rocks; then, expelling her breath and kicking upwards, she rushed head-down; the water closed round, the stone rushed past and she struggled up into the air. She was inside the walls.

And so is he, she thought. For somebody had cleaned the place up. What she remembered as choked with stone rubbish (she had used the place for purposes of her own a few years back) was bare and neat and clean; all was square, all was orderly, and someone had cut stone steps from the level of the water to the most beautifully precise archway in the world. But of course she should not have been able to see any of this at all. The place should have been in absolute darkness. Instead, on either side of the arch was a dim glow, with a narrow beam of light going between them; she could see dancing in it the dust-motes that are never absent from this earth, not even from air that has lain quiet within the rock of a wizard's mansion for uncountable years. Up to her neck in the ocean, this barbarian woman then stood very quietly and thoughtfully for several minutes. Then she dove down into the sea again, and when she came up her knotted cloak was full of the tiny crabs that cling to the rocks along the seacoast of Ourdh. One she killed and the others she suspended captive in the sea; bits of the blood and flesh of the first she smeared carefully below the two sources of that narrow beam of light; then she crept back into the sea and loosed the others at the very bottom step, diving underwater as the first of the hurrying little creatures reached the arch. There was a brilliant flash of light, then another, and then darkness. Alyx waited. Hoisting herself out of the water, she walked through the arch—not quickly, but not without nervousness. The crabs were pushing and quarreling over their dead cousin. Several climbed over the sources of the beam, *pulling,* she thought, *the crabs over his eyes.* However he saw, he had seen nothing. The first alarm had been sprung.

Wizards' castles—and their country residences—have every right to be infested with all manner of horrors, but Alyx saw nothing. The passage wound on, going fairly constantly upward, and as it rose it grew lighter until every now and then she could see a kind of lighter shape against the blackness and a few stars. These were windows. There was no sound but her own breathing and once in a while the complaining rustle of one or two little creatures she had inadvertently carried with her in a corner of her cloak. When she stopped she heard nothing. The fat man was either very quiet or very far away. She hoped it was quietness. She slung the cloak over her shoulder and began the climb again.

Then she ran into a wall.

This shocked her, but she gathered herself together and tried the experiment again. She stepped back, then walked forward and again she ran into a wall, not rock but something at once elastic and unyielding, and at the very same moment someone said (as it seemed to her, inside her head) *You cannot get through.*

Alyx swore, religiously. She fell back and nearly lost her balance. She put out one hand and again she touched something impalpable, tingling and elastic; again the voice sounded close behind her ear, with an uncomfortable, frightening intimacy as if she were speaking to herself: *You cannot get through.* "Can't I!" she shouted, quite losing her nerve, and drew her sword; it plunged forward without the slightest resistance, but something again stopped her bare hand and the voice repeated with idiot softness, over and over *You cannot get through. You cannot get through—*

"Who are you!" said she, but there was no answer. She backed down the stairs, sword drawn, and waited. Nothing happened. Round her the stone walls glimmered, barely visible, for the moon was rising outside; patiently she waited, pressing the corner of her cloak with her foot, for as it lay on the floor one of the crabs had chewed his way to freedom and had given her ankle a tremendous nip on the way out. The light increased.

There was nothing there. The crab, who had scuttled busily ahead on the landing of the stair, seemed to come to the place himself and stood there, fiddling. There was absolutely nothing there. Then Alyx, who had been watching the little animal with something close to hopeless calm, gave an exclamation and threw herself flat on the stairs—for the crab had begun to climb upward between floor and ceiling and what it was climbing on was nothing. Tears forced themselves to her eyes. Swimming behind her lids she could see her husband's face, appearing first in one place, then in another, as if frozen on the black box the fat man had showed her the first day they met. She laid herself on the stone and cried. Then she got up, for the face seemed to settle on the other side of the landing and it occurred to her that she must go through. She was still crying. She took off one of her sandals and pushed it through the something-nothing (the crab still climbed in the air with perfect comfort). It went through easily. She grew nauseated at the thought of touching the crab and the thing it climbed on, but she put one hand involuntarily over her face and made a grab with the other (*You cannot* said the voice). When she had got the struggling animal thoroughly in her grasp, she dashed it against the rocky side wall of the tunnel and flung it forward with all her strength. It fell clattering twenty feet further on.

The distinction then, she thought, *is between life and death,* and she sat down hopelessly on the steps to figure this out, for the problem of dying so as to get through and yet getting through without dying, struck her as insoluble. Twenty feet down the tunnel (the spot was in darkness and she could not see what it was) something rustled. It sounded remarkably like a crab that had been stunned and was now recovering, for these animals think of nothing but food and disappointments only seem to give them fresh strength for the search. Alyx gaped into the dark. She felt the hairs rise on the back of her neck. She would have given a great deal to see into that spot, for it seemed to her that she now guessed at the principle of the fat man's demon, which kept out any conscious mind—as it had spoken in hers—but perhaps would let through . . . She pondered. This cynical woman had been a religious enthusiast before circumstances forced her into a drier way of thinking; thus it was that she now slung her cloak ahead of her on the ground to break her fall and leaned deliberately, from head to feet, into the horrid, springy net she could not see. Closing her eyes and pressing the fingers of both hands over an artery in the back of her neck, she began to repeat to herself a formula that she had learned in those prehistoric years, one that has to be altered slightly each time it is repeated—almost as effective a self-hypnotic device as counting backward. And the voice, too, whispering over and over *You*

*cannot get through, you cannot get through—cannot
—cannot—*

Something gave her a terrific shock through teeth, bones and flesh, and she woke to find the floor of the landing tilted two inches from her eyes. One knee was twisted under her and the left side of her face ached dizzily, warm and wet under a cushion of numbness. She guessed that her face had been laid open in the fall and her knee sprained, if not broken.

But she was through.

She found the fat man in a room at the very top of the tower, sitting in a pair of shorts in a square of light at the end of a corridor; and, as she made her way limping towards him, he grew (unconscious and busy) to the size of a human being, until at last she stood inside the room, vaguely aware of blood along her arm and a stinging on her face where she had tried to wipe her wound with her cloak. The room was full of machinery. The fat man (he had been jiggling some little arrangement of wires and blocks on his lap) looked up, saw her, registered surprise and then broke into a great grin.

"So it's you," he said.

She said nothing. She put one arm along the wall to steady herself.

"You are amazing," he said, "perfectly amazing. Come here," and he rose and sent his stool spinning away with a touch. He came up to where she stood, wet and shivering, staining the floor and wall, and for a long minute he studied her. Then he said softly:

"Poor animal. Poor little wretch."

Her breathing was ragged. She glanced rapidly about her, taking in the size of the room (it broadened to encompass the whole width of the tower) and the four great windows that opened to the four winds, and the strange things in the shadows: multitudes of little tables, boards hung on the walls, knobs and switches and winking lights innumerable. But she did not move or speak.

"Poor animal," he said again. He walked back and surveyed her contemptuously, both arms akimbo, and then he said, "Do you believe the world was once a lump of rock?"

"Yes," she said.

"Many years ago," he said, "many more years than your mind can comprehend, before there were trees—or cities—or women—I came to this lump of rock. Do you believe that?"

She nodded.

"I came here," said he gently, "in the satisfaction of a certain hobby, and I made all that you see in this room— all the little things you were looking at a moment ago— and I made the tower, too. Sometimes I make it new inside and sometimes I make it look old. Do you understand that, little one?"

She said nothing.

"And when the whim hits me," he said, "I make it new and comfortable and I settle into it, and once I have settled into it I begin to practice my hobby. Do you know what my hobby is?" He chuckled.

"My hobby, little one," he said, "came from this tower and this machinery, for this machinery can reach all over the world and then things happen exactly as I choose. Now do you know what my hobby is? My hobby is world-making. I make worlds, little one."

She took a quick breath, like a sigh, but she did not speak. He smiled at her.

"Poor beast," he said, "you are dreadfully cut about the face and I believe you have sprained one of your limbs. Hunting animals are always doing that. But it won't last. Look," he said, "look again," and he moved one fat hand in a slow circle around him. "It is I, little one," he said, "who made everything that your eyes have ever rested on. Apes and peacocks, tides and times" (he laughed) "and the fire and the rain. I made you. I made your husband. Come," and he ambled off into the shadows. The circle of light that had rested on him when

Alyx first entered the room now followed him, continually keeping him at its center, and although her hair rose to see it, she forced herself to follow, limping in pain past the tables, through stacks of tubing and wire and between square shapes the size of stoves. The light fled always before her. Then he stopped, and as she came up to the light, he said:

"You know, I am not angry at you."

Alyx winced as her foot struck something, and grabbed her knee.

"No, I am not," he said. "It has been delightful—except for tonight, which demonstrates, between ourselves, that the whole thing was something of a mistake and shouldn't be indulged in again—but you must understand that I cannot allow a creation of mine, a paring of my fingernail, if you take my meaning, to rebel in this silly fashion." He grinned. "No, no," he said, "that I cannot do. And so" (here he picked up a glass cube from the table in back of him) "I have decided" (here he joggled the cube a little) "that tonight—why, my dear, what is the matter with you? You are standing there with the veins in your fists knotted as if you would like to strike me, even though your knee is giving you a great deal of trouble just at present and you would be better employed in supporting some of your weight with your hands or I am very much mistaken." And he held out to her—though not far enough for her to reach it—the glass cube, which contained an image of her husband in little, unnaturally sharp, like a picture let into crystal. "See?" he said. "When I turn the lever to the right, the little beasties rioting in his bones grow ever more calm and that does him good. A great deal of good. But when I turn the lever to the left—"

"Devil!" said she.

"Ah, I've gotten something out of you at last!" he said, coming closer. "At last you know! Ah, little one, many and many a time I have seen you wondering whether the world might not be better off if you stabbed me in the

back, eh? But you can't, you know. Why don't you try it?"
He patted her on the shoulder. "Here I am, you see, quite
close enough to you, peering, in fact, into those tragic,
blazing eyes—wouldn't it be natural to try and put an
end to me? But you can't, you know. You'd be puzzled if
you tried. I wear an armor plate, little beast, that any
beast might envy, and you could throw me from a ten-
thousand-foot mountain, or fry me in a furnace, or do a
hundred and one other deadly things to me without the
least effect. My armor plate has *in-er-tial dis-crim-in-a-
tion*, little savage, which means that it lets nothing too
fast and nothing too heavy get through. So you cannot
hurt me at all. To murder me, you would have to strike
me, but that is too fast and too heavy and so is the
ground that hits me when I fall and so is fire. Come
here."

She did not move.

"Come here, monkey," he said. "I'm going to kill your
man and then I will send you away; though since you
operate so well in the dark, I think I'll bless you and
make that your permanent condition. What do you think
you're doing?" for she had put her fingers to her sleeve;
and while he stood, smiling a little with the cube in his
hand, she drew her dagger and fell upon him, stabbing
him again and again.

"There," he said complacently, "do you see?"

"I see," she said hoarsely, finding her tongue.

"Do you understand?"

"I understand," she said.

"Then move off," he said, "I have got to finish," and
he brought the cube up to the level of his eyes. She saw
her man, behind the glass as in a refracting prism, break
into a multiplicity of images; she saw him reach out gro-
tesquely to the surface; she saw his fingertips strike at
the surface as if to erupt into the air; and while the fat
man took the lever between thumb and forefinger and—
prissily and precisely, his lips pursed into wrinkles, prepared to move it all the way to the left—

She put her fingers in his eyes and then, taking advantage of his pain and blindness, took the cube from him and bent him over the edge of a table in such a way as to break his back. This all took place inside the body. His face worked spasmodically, one eye closed and unclosed in a hideous parody of a wink, his fingers paddled feebly on the tabletop and he fell to the floor.

"My dear!" he gasped.

She looked at him expressionlessly.

"Help me," he whispered, "eh?" His fingers fluttered. "Over there," he said eagerly, "medicines. Make me well, eh? Good and fast. I'll give you half."

"All," she said.

"Yes, yes, all," he said breathlessly, "all—explain all —fascinating hobby—spend most of my time in this room—get the medicine—"

"First show me," she said, "how to turn it off."

"Off?" he said. He watched her, bright-eyed.

"First," she said patiently, "I will turn it all off. And then I will cure you."

"No," he said, "no, no! Never!" She knelt down beside him.

"Come," she said softly, "do you think I want to destroy it? I am as fascinated by it as you are. I only want to make sure you can't do anything to me, that's all. You must explain it all first until I am master of it, too, and then we will turn it on."

"No, no," he repeated suspiciously.

"You must," she said, "or you'll die. What do you think I plan to do? I have to cure you, because otherwise how can I learn to work all this? But I must be safe, too. Show me how to turn it off."

He pointed, doubtfully.

"Is that it?" she said.

"Yes," he said, "but—"

"Is that it?"

"Yes, but—no—wait!" for Alyx sprang to her feet and fetched from his stool the pillow on which he had been sitting, the purpose of which he did not at first seem to comprehend, but then his eyes went wide with horror; for she had got the pillow in order to smother him, and that is just what she did.

When she got to her feet, her legs were trembling. Stumbling and pressing both hands together as if in prayer to subdue their shaking, she took the cube that held her husband's picture and carefully—oh, how carefully!—turned the lever to the right. Then she began to sob. It was not the weeping of grief, but a kind of reaction and triumph, all mixed; in the middle of that eerie room she stood, and threw her head back and yelled. The light burned steadily on. In the shadows she found the fat man's master switch, and leaning against the wall, put one finger—only one—on it and caught her breath. Would the world end? She did not know. After a few minutes' search she found a candle and flint hidden away in a cupboard and with this she made herself a light; then, with eyes closed, with a long shudder, she leaned—no, sagged —against the switch, and stood for a long moment, expecting and believing nothing.

But the world did not end. From outside came the wind and the sound of the sea-wash (though louder now, as if some indistinct and not quite audible humming had just ended) and inside fantastic shadows leapt about the candle—the lights had gone out. Alyx began to laugh, catching her breath. She set the candle down and searched until she found a length of metal tubing that stood against the wall, and then she went from machine to machine, smashing, prying, tearing, toppling tables and breaking controls. Then she took the candle in her unsteady hand and stood over the body of the fat man, a phantasmagoric lump on the floor, badly lit at last. Her shadow loomed on the wall. She leaned over him and studied his face, that face that had made out of agony and death the most appalling trivialities. She thought:

Make the world? You hadn't the imagination. You didn't even make these machines; that shiny finish is for

*customers, not craftsmen, and controls that work by little
pictures are for children. You are a child yourself, a child
and a horror, and I would ten times rather be subject to
your machinery than master of it.*

Aloud she said:

"Never confuse the weapon and the arm," and taking
the candle, she went away and left him in the dark.

She got home at dawn and, as her man lay asleep in
bed, it seemed to her that he was made out of the light of
the dawn that streamed through his fingers and his hair,
irradiating him with gold. She kissed him and he opened
his eyes.

"You've come home," he said.

"So I have," said she.

"I fought all night," she added, "with the Old Man of
the Mountain," for you must know that this demon is a
legend in Ourdh; he is the god of this world who dwells
in a cave containing the whole world in little, and from
his cave he rules the fates of men.

"Who won?" said her husband, laughing, for in the
sunrise when everything is suffused with light it is difficult
to see the seriousness of injuries.

"I did!" said she. "The man is dead." She smiled, splitting open the wound on her cheek, which began to bleed
afresh. "He died," she said, "for two reasons only: because he was a fool. And because we are not."

And all the birds in the courtyard broke out shouting
at once.

Like the late Harold Ross of The New Yorker and most other editors, I am reluctant to print any story I don't understand. "The Changeling" appears here, nevertheless.

In my book of critical essays, In Search of Wonder, I made a distinction between stories that make sense and those that mean something. I am unable to "make sense" out of this one—to make it aad up neatly and come out even—but I strongly feel that it means something, just as Kafka's The Trial or Shirley Jackson's "The Lottery" does.

This haunting story is Gene Wolfe's second for Orbit; his first was "Trip, Trap," in Orbit 2.

The Changeling

by Gene Wolfe

I suppose whoever finds these papers will be amazed at
the simplicity of their author, who put them under a stone
instead of into a mailbox or a filing cabinet or even a cor-
nerstone—these being the places where most think it wise
to store up their writings. But consider, is it not wiser to
put papers like these into the gut of a dry cave as I have
done?

For if a building is all it should be, the future will
spare it for a shrine; and if your children's sons think it
not worth keeping, will they think the letters of the build-
ers worth reading? Yet that would be a surer way than a
filing cabinet. Answer truly: Did you ever know of papers
to be read again once they entered one of these, save
when some clerk drew them out by number? And who
would seek for these?

There is a great, stone-beaked, hook-billed snapping
turtle living under the bank here, and in the spring, when
the waterfowl have nested and brooded, he swims beneath their chicks more softly than any shadow. Sometimes they peep once when he takes their legs, and so
they have more of life than these sheets would have once
the clacking cast iron jaw of a mailbox closed on them.

Have you ever noted how eager it is to close when you
have pulled out your hand? You cannot write *The Future*
on the outside of an envelope; the box would cross that
out and stamp *Dead Letter Office* in its place.

Still, I have a tale to tell; and a tale untold is one sort of crime:

I was in the army, serving in Korea, when my father died. That was before the North invaded, and I was supposed to be helping a captain teach demolition to the ROK soldiers. The army gave me compassionate leave when the hospital in Buffalo sent a telegram saying how sick he was. I suppose everyone moved as fast as they could, I know I did, but he died while I was flying across the Pacific. I looked into his coffin where the blue silk lining came up to his hard, brown cheeks and crowded his working shoulders; and went back to Korea. He was the last family I had, and things changed for me then.

There isn't much use in my making a long story of what happened afterward; you can read it all in the court-martial proceedings. I was one of the ones who stayed behind in China, neither the first nor the last to change his mind a second time and come home. I was also one of the ones who had to stand trial; let's say that some of the men who had been in the prison camp with me remembered things differently. You don't have to like it.

While I was in Ft. Leavenworth I started thinking about how it was before my mother died, how my father could bend a big nail with his fingers when we lived in Cassonsville and I went to the Immaculate Conception School five days a week. We left the month before I was supposed to start the fifth grade, I think.

When I got out I decided to go back there and look around before I tried to get a job. I had four hundred dollars I had put in Soldier's Deposit before the war, and I knew a lot about living cheap. You learn that in China.

I wanted to see if the Kanakessee River still looked as smooth as it used to, and if the kids I had played softball with had married each other, and what they were like now. Somehow the old part of my life seemed to have broken away, and I wanted to go back and look at that piece. There was a fat boy who was tongue-tied and laughed at everything, but I had forgotten his name. I remembered our pitcher, Ernie Cotha, who was in my grade at school and had buck teeth and freckles; his sister played center field for us when we couldn't get anybody else, and closed her eyes until the ball thumped the ground in front of her. Peter Palmieri always wanted to play Vikings or something like that, and pretty often made the rest of us want to too. His big sister Maria bossed and mothered us all from the towering dignity of thirteen. Somewhere in the background another Palmieri, a baby brother named Paul, followed us around watching everything we did with big, brown eyes. He must have been about four then; he never talked, but we thought he was an awful pest.

I was lucky in my rides and moved out of Kansas pretty well. After a couple of days I figured I would be spending the next night in Cassonsville, but it seemed as though I had run out of welcomes outside a little hamburger joint where the state route branched off the federal highway. I had been holding out my thumb nearly three hours before a guy in an old Ford station wagon offered me a lift. I'd mumbled, "Thanks," and tossed my AWOL bag in back before I ever got a good look at him. It was Ernie Cotha, and I knew him right away—even though a dentist had done something to his teeth so they didn't push his lip out any more. I had a little fun with him before he got me placed, and then we got into a regular school reunion mood talking about the old times.

I remember we passed a little barefoot kid standing alongside the road, and Ernie said, "You recollect how Paul always got in the way, and one time we rubbed his hair with a cow pile? You told me next day how you caught blazes from Mama Palmieri about it."

I'd forgotten, but it all came back as soon as he mentioned it. "You know," I said, "it was a shame the way we treated that boy. He thought we were big shots, and we made him suffer for it."

"It didn't hurt him any," Ernie said. "Wait till you see him; I bet he could lick us both."

"The family still live in town?"

"Oh sure." Ernie let the car drift off the blacktop a little, and it threw up a spurt of dust and gravel before he got it back on. "Nobody leaves Cassonsville." He took his eyes from the road for a moment to look at me. "You knew Maria's old Doc Witte's nurse now? And the old people have a little motel on the edge of the fairgrounds. You want me to drop you there, Pete?"

I asked him how the rates were, and he said they were low enough, so, since I'd have to bunk down somewhere, I told him that would be all right. We were quiet then for five or six miles, before Ernie started up again.

"Say, you remember the big fight you two had? Down by the river. You wanted to tie a rock to a frog and throw him in, and Maria wouldn't let you. That was a real scrap."

"It wasn't Maria," I told him, "that was Peter."

"You're nuts," Ernie said. "That must have been twenty years ago. Peter wasn't even born then."

"You must be thinking of another Peter," I said. "I mean Peter Palmieri, Maria's brother."

Ernie stared at me until I thought he was going to run us into the ditch. "That's who I mean too," he said, "but little Peter's only a kid eight, maybe nine." He glanced back at the road. "You're thinking of Paul, only it was Maria you had the fight with; Paul was just a toddler."

We were quiet again for a few minutes after that, and it gave me time to remember that tussle on the river bank. I recalled that four or five of us had walked up to the point where we always tied the skiff we used to cross over to our rocky, useless island in the middle of the channel. We meant to play pirates or something, but the skiff had dragged loose from its moorings and was gone. Peter had tried to get the rest of us to search downstream for it, but everyone was too lazy. It was one of those hot, still summer days when the dust floats in the air; the days

that make you think of threshing. I caught a frog somehow and hit upon the idea for an experiment.

Then I remembered that Ernie was at least partially
right. Maria had tried to stop me and I had hit her in the
eye with a stone. But that wasn't the big fight. It was
Peter who came to avenge Maria then, Peter with whom I
rolled snarling and scratching, trying to get a grip on his
sweat-slick body in the prickly weeds. Ernie was right
about Paul's being no more than an infant, and there had
been a scrap with Maria; but it was Peter who'd finally
made me cut the string from the frog's leg and let it go.
Side by side we had watched the little green animal hop
back toward the water, and then, when it was only one
jump away from dear safety, I had lashed out and suddenly, swiftly, driven the broad blade of my scout knife
through him and pinned him to the mud.

The Palmieris' place was called The Cassonsville Tour-
ist Lodge. There were ten white cottages and a house
with a café jutting out of the front to support a big sign
that said *EAT* like Buddha commanding the grasshopper.

Mama Palmieri surprised me by recognizing me at
once and smothering me with kisses. She herself had
hardly changed at all. Her hair had gone gray at the temples, but most of it was still the glossy black it had been;
and while she had always been fat, she was no fatter now.
Maybe not quite so solid looking. I don't think Papa
really remembered me, but he gave me one of his rare
smiles.

He was a small, dark, philosophical man who seldom
spoke, and I suppose people meeting the two of them for
the first time would assume that Mama dominated her
husband. The truth was that she regarded him as infalli-
ble in every crisis. And for practical purposes Mama was
almost right; he had the inexhaustible patience and rock-
bound common sense of a Sicilian burro—all the qualities
that have made that tough, diminutive animal the tradi-
tional companion of wandering friars and desert rats.

The Palmieris wanted me to stay in Maria's room (she

had gone to Chicago to attend some sort of nurses' convention and was not due back until the end of the week) as a guest, and insisted that I eat with the family. I made them rent me a cabin instead at five dollars a night—which they swore was the full rate—but I gave in on the eating. We were still talking in that disjointed way people do on these occasions when Paul came in.

I would not have recognized him if I'd met him on the street, but I liked him at first sight; a big, dark, solemn kid with a handsome profile he had never discovered and probably never would.

After Mama made the introductions she started worrying about dinner and wondering when Peter would get home. Paul reassured her by saying he'd driven past Peter walking with a gang of kids as he'd come out from town. He said he'd offered his brother a lift but had been turned down.

Something about the way he said it gave me the willies. I remembered what Ernie had said about Peter being younger than Paul, and somehow Paul gave the same impression. He was wearing a college sweater and had the half cocky, half unsure mannerisms of a boy trying to be a man, yet he seemed to be talking about someone much younger.

After a while we heard the screen door slam and light, quick steps coming in. When I saw him I knew I had been expecting it all along. It was Peter, and he was perhaps eight years old. Not just another Italian-looking kid; but Peter, with his sharp chin and black eyes. He didn't seem to recall me at all, and Mama bragged about how not many women could bear healthy sons at fifty like she had. I went to bed early that night.

Naturally I had been keyed up all evening waiting to hear something that would show they knew about me; but when I fell asleep I was thinking about Peter, and I hadn't been thinking about anything else for a long time.

The next day was Saturday, and since Paul had the day off from his summer job he offered to drive me around town. He had a '54 Chevy he had pretty much rebuilt himself, and he was very proud of it.

After we had seen all the usual things, which didn't take long in Cassonsville, I asked him to take me to the island in the river where we had played as boys. We had to walk about a mile because the road doesn't come close to the river at that point, but there was a path the kids had made. Grasshoppers fled in waves before us through the dry grass.

When we got to the water Paul said, "That's funny, there's usually a little boat here the kids use to get out to the island."

I was looking at the island, and I saw the skiff tied to a bush at the edge of the water. It looked like the same one we had used when I was a kid myself, and who knows, maybe it was. The island itself interested me more. It was a good deal closer to shore—in fact, the Kanakessee was a good deal narrower—than I had remembered, but I had expected that since everything in Cassonsville was smaller including the town itself. What surprised me was that the island was bigger, if anything. There was a high point, almost a hill, in the center that sloped down and then up to a bluff on the upstream end, and trailed a long piece of wasteland downstream. Altogether it must have covered four or five acres.

In a few minutes we saw a boy on the island, and Paul yelled across the water for him to row the boat over to us. He did, and Paul rowed the three of us back. I remember I was afraid the little skiff would founder under the load; the silent water was no more than an inch from pouring over the sides, despite the boy's bailing with a rusty can to lighten the boat of its bilge.

On the island we found three more boys, including Peter. There were some wooden swords, made by nailing a short slat crosswise to a longer, thrust into the ground; but none of the boys were holding them. Seeing Peter there, just as he used to be when I was a kid myself, made me search the faces of the other boys to see if I could find someone else I had known among them. I couldn't; they were just ordinary kids. What I am trying to say is that I felt too tall out here to be a real person, and out of place in the only place where I really wanted to be. Maybe it was because the boys were sulky, angry at having their game interrupted and afraid of being laughed at. Maybe it was because every tree and rock and bush and berry tangle was familiar and unaltered—but unremembered before I saw it.

From the bank the island had seemed nearer, though larger, than I recalled. Now, somehow, there was much more water between it and the shore. The illusion was so odd that I tapped Paul on the shoulder and said, "I'll bet you can't throw a rock from here to the other side."

He grinned at me and said, "What'll you bet?"

Peter said, "He can't do it. Nobody can." It was the first time any of the boys had spoken above a mumble.

I had been planning to pay for Paul's gasoline anyway, so I said that if he did it I'd get his tank filled at the first station we came to on the way home.

The stone arced out and out until it seemed more like an arrow than a pebble, and at last dropped into the water with a splash. As nearly as I could judge it was still about thirty feet from the bank.

"There," Paul said, "I told you I could do it."

"I thought it dropped short," I said.

"The sun must have been in your eyes." Paul sounded positive. "It dropped four foot up the bank." Picking up another rock, he tossed it confidently from one hand to the other. "If you want me to, I'll do it over."

For a second I couldn't believe my ears. Paul hadn't struck me as someone who would try to collect a bet he hadn't won. I looked at the four boys. Usually there's nothing that will fire up a boy like a bet or the offer of a prize, but these still resented our intrusion too much to talk. All of them were looking at Paul, however, with the deep contempt a normal kid feels for a welcher.

I said, "O.K., you won," to Paul and got a boy to come with us in the skiff so he could row it back.

When we reached the car, Paul mentioned that there was a baseball game that afternoon, Class "A" ball, at the county seat; so we drove over and watched the game. That is, I sat and stared at the field, but when it was over I couldn't have told you whether the final score was nothing to nothing or twenty to five. On the way home I bought Paul's gas.

It was suppertime when we got back, and after supper Paul and Papa Palmieri and I sat out on the porch and drank cans of beer. We talked baseball for a little while, then Paul left. I told Papa a few stories about Paul hanging around with us older kids when he was small, then about me fighting with Peter over the frog, and waited for him to correct me.

He sat without speaking for a long time. Finally I said, "What's the matter?"

He re-lit his cigar and said, "You know all about it." It wasn't a question.

I told him I didn't really know anything about it, but that up to that minute I was beginning to think I was losing my mind.

He said, "You want to hear?" His voice was completely mechanical except for the trace of Italian accent. I said I did.

"Mama and me came here from Chicago when Maria was just a little baby, you know?"

I told him I had heard something about it.

"I have a good job, that's why we come to this town. Foreman at the brick works."

I said I knew that too. He had held that job while I was a kid in Cassonsville.

"We rented a little white house down on Front Street, and unpacked our stuff. Even bought some new. Everybody knew I had a good job; my credit was good. We'd been in the town couple months, I guess, when I came home from work one night and find Mama and the baby with this strange boy. Mama's holding little Maria in her lap and saying, 'Look there, Maria, that's-a your big brother.' I think maybe Mama's gone crazy, or playing a joke on me, or something. That night the kids eat with us like there was nothing strange at all."

"What did you do?" I asked him.

"I didn't do nothing. Nine times outa ten that's the best thing you can do. I wait and keep my eyes open. Night time comes and the boy goes to a little room upstairs we weren't going to use and goes to sleep. He's got an army cot there, clothes in the closet, school books, everything. Mama says we ought to get him a real bed soon when she sees me looking in there."

"Was Mama the only one . . . ?"

Papa lit a fresh cigar and I realized that it was growing dark and that both of us had been pitching our voices lower than usual.

"Everybody," Papa said. "The next day after work I go to the nuns at the school. I think I'll tell them what he looks like; maybe they know who he is."

"What did they say?" I asked him.

"They say, 'Oh, you're Peter Palmieri's papa, he's such a nice boy,' soon's I tell them who I am. Everybody's like that." He was silent for a long time, then he added, "When *my* Papa writes next from the old country he says, 'How's my little Peter?' "

"That was all there was to it?"

The old man nodded. "He stays with us, and he's a good boy—better than Paul or Maria. But he never grows up. First he's Maria's big brother. Then he's her twin brother. Then little brother. Now he's Paul's little brother. Pretty soon he'll be too young to belong to Mama and me and then he'll leave, I think. You're the only one besides me who ever noticed. You played with them when you're a kid, huh?"

I told him, "Yes."

We sat on the porch for a half hour or so longer, but neither of us wanted to talk any more. When I got up to leave Papa said, "One thing. Three times I get holy water from the priest an' pour it on him while he sleeps. Nothing happens, no blisters, no screaming, nothing."

The next day was Sunday. I put on my best clothes, a clean sport shirt and good slacks, and hitched a ride to town with a truck driver who'd stopped for an early coffee at the café. I knew the nuns at Immaculate Conception would all go to the first couple of masses at the church, but since I had wanted to get away from the motel before the Palmieris grabbed me to go with them I had to leave early. I spent three hours loafing about the town—everything was closed—then went to the little convent and rang the bell.

A young nun I had never seen before answered and took me to see the Mother Superior, and it turned out to be Sister Leona, who had taught the third grade. She hadn't changed much; nuns don't, it's the covered hair and never wearing makeup, I think. Anyway, as soon as I saw her I remembered her as though I had just left her class, but I don't think she placed me, even though I told her who I was. When I was through explaining I asked her to let me see the records on Peter Palmieri, and she wouldn't. I'd wanted to see if they could possibly have a whole file drawer of cards and reports going back twenty years or more on one boy, but though I pleaded and yelled and finally threatened she kept saying that each student's records were confidential and could be shown only with the parent's permission.

Then I changed my tactics. I remembered perfectly well that when we were in the fourth grade a class picture had been taken. I could even recall the day, how hot it was, and how the photographer had ducked in and out of his cloth, looking like a bent-over nun when he was aiming the camera. I asked Sister Leona if I could look at that. She hesitated a minute and then agreed and had the young sister bring a big album that she told me had all the class pictures since the school was founded. I asked for the fourth grade of nineteen forty-four and after some shuffling she found it.

We were ranged in alternate columns of boys and girls, just as I had remembered. Each boy had a girl on either side of him but another boy in front and in back. Peter, I was certain, had stood directly behind me one step higher on the school steps, and though I couldn't think of their names I recalled the faces of the girls to my right and left perfectly.

The picture was a little dim and faded now, and having seen the school building on my way to the convent I was surprised at how much newer it had looked then. I found the spot where I had stood, second row from the back and about three spaces over from our teacher Sister Therese, but my face wasn't there. Between the two girls, tiny in the photograph, was the sharp, dark face of Peter Palmieri. No one stood behind him, and the boy in front was Ernie Cotha. I ran my eyes over the list of names at the bottom of the picture and his name was there, but mine was not.

I don't know what I said to Sister Leona or how I got out of the convent. I only remember walking very fast through the almost empty Sunday-morning streets until the sign in front of the newspaper office caught my eye. The sun was reflected from the gilded lettering and the plate glass window in a blinding glare, but I could see dimly the figures of two men moving about inside. I kicked the door until one of them opened it and let me into the ink-scented room. I didn't recognize either of them, yet the expectancy of the silent, oiled presses in back was as familiar as anything in Cassonsville, unchanged since I had come in with my father to buy the ad to sell our place.

I was too tired to fence with them. Something had been taken out of me in the convent and I could feel my empty belly with a little sour coffee in it. I said, "Listen to me please, sir. There was a boy named Pete Palmer; he was born in this town. He stayed behind when the prisoners were exchanged at Panmunjom and went to Red China and worked in a textile mill there. They sent him to prison when he came back. He'd changed his name after he left here, but that wouldn't make any difference; there'll be a lot about him because he was a local boy. Can I look in your files under August and September of 1959? Please?"

They looked at each other and then at me. One was an old man with badly fitting false teeth and a green eye-shade like a movie newspaperman; the other was fat and tough looking with dull, stupid eyes. Finally the old man said, "There wasn't no Cassonsville boy stayed with the Communists. I'da remembered a thing like that."

I said, "Can I look, please?"

He shrugged his shoulders. "It's fifty cents an hour to use them files, and you can't tear out nothing or take nothing out with you, understand?"

I gave him two quarters and he led me back to the morgue. There was nothing, nothing at all. There was nothing for 1953 when the exchange had taken place either. I tried to look up my birth announcement then, but there were no files before 1945; the old man out front said they'd been "burnt up when the old shop burned."

I went outside then and stood in the sun awhile. Then I went back to the motel and got my bag and went out to the island. There were no kids this time; it was very lonely and very peaceful. I poked around a bit and found this cave on the south side, then lay down on the grass and smoked my last two cigarettes and listened to the river and looked up at the sky. Before I knew it, it had started to get dark and I knew I'd better begin the trip home. When it was too dark to see the bank across the river I went into this cave to sleep.

I think I had really known from the first that I was never going to leave the island again. The next morning I untied the skiff and let it drift away on the current, though I knew the boys would find it hung up on some snag and bring it back.

How do I live? People bring me things, and I do a good deal of fishing—even through the ice in winter. Then there are blackberries and walnuts here on the island. I think a lot, and if you do that right it's better than the things people who come to see me sometimes tell me they couldn't do without.

You'd be surprised at how many do come to talk to me. One or two almost every week. They bring me fish-hooks and sometimes a blanket or a sack of potatoes and some of them tell me they wish to God they were me.

The boys still come, of course. I wasn't counting them when I said one or two people. Papa was wrong. Peter still has the same last name as always and I guess now he always will, but the boys don't call him by it much.

In 1966 I was privileged to be one of the judges of a computer story contest sponsored by Data Processing magazine. The stories were all interesting, although most of them were unprofessionally written; some were very good, and as a group they presented a remarkably unanimous picture of the near future. (A computerized bureaucracy is going to run our lives, and there isn't a damn thing we can do about it.)

Doris Buck is a prime exhibit in my gallery of writers who have never grown up. Although she is a grandmother, well into the age of discretion, she is one of the least bored people I know; she is alert, interested, full of enthusiasm. (And her husband, Richard S. Buck, who is in his seventies and has a white beard to prove it, is just the same.)

The author did not enter this story in the computer contest, although I urged her to (she said she would rather sell it to Orbit, bless her heart); but in my opinion it is better than any of the winners, as well as much funnier.

Why They Mobbed The White House

by Doris Pitkin Buck

"Hubert was glad he lived in an age when they still had jet transport. The big tunnels got you across the continent faster, but the two-hour jet trip gave you a chance to enjoy the landscape. And Lila loved to hear his description of the Rockies that looked for the whole of their length like a shelf canted over toward the west. Hubert and Lila planned to vacation there sometime. He saved up his credits conscientiously. But Lila's health had been unpredictable ever since Hubert had volunteered for the late East Asian War.

"Even when Hubert topped his Congressional Medal of Honor and won the Legion of Purity's Silver Halo for being the only private in the entire Third Expeditionary Force never to have entered a hot spot in Singapore, Saigon, Shanghai or Tokyo, Lila still showed vague, distressing symptoms. When more decorations were showered on him, she'd take days off from the family record-keeping that had once been Hubert's chore. She'd spend this free time writing ecstatic letters. The itches, the spots, the hive-like bumps, the vein distensions with their sub-aches let up temporarily. But once she was back at the usual secretarial-computation routine that had succeeded housework as the Number One domestic bane, she was as physically wretched as ever, even in her pride.

"Hubert, who worshiped her as Arthurian knights adored their ladies, put a great deal of thought on her problem. If she met him on his return from business trips, an opaque veil over her once pert nose and swollen coralline mouth, Hubert saddened. He had imagination. He realized what having to hide her face meant to Lila. He kissed her on the temple. Even with this Victorian salutation, Hubert would feel Lila catch her breath. It drew a little of the veil right into her mouth. They tried to laugh that off as something comic. But their eyes moistened with the tragedy of it.

"When Hubert reached his house after this business trip, Lila could not get out of bed. Her ankles were dropsical with edema. Far worse, her eyes were swollen shut. But this time her mouth was visible. Her rosy lips under her temporarily sightless eyes murmured, 'Darling, do you know what day it is?'

"Hubert searched his prodigious memory for a forgotten anniversary. He knew perfectly well the day was April 7. But they'd been married in June. They were engaged on Valentine's Day. They had both been born on September 9. It wasn't Mother's Day. It wasn't Father's Day. It wasn't Remember-the-Grandparents Day. Nor Armistice Day. Nor Unknown Soldier's Day. Nor Adopt-a-Veteran Day. Nor Corsage Day. Nor Let's-Eat-Out Day. Nor National Safety Day. It was only April 7, which had the distinction of being no particular day.

"Hubert was at a loss. He fell back on a true and tried tactic. He said, 'What have I done?'

" 'Nothing. *I've* failed *you*. Ever since you enlisted,' she said, scratching, 'I've made out our income tax. I work on it a little every week in the year.' She scratched again. 'But I'm still only on the seventy-third page. I'm lying here blind. And the returns are due on April 15.'

" 'Let it go,' Hubert cried. 'I can afford the penalty.'

" 'You've forgotten, Hubert. Oh!' Lila refrained from scratching but the effort hurt. 'Congress amended the penalty clause when you were overseas. It carries a jail sentence now. Optional with the IRS, but it is there.'

" 'Don't worry. I'll make it out the way I used to.'

" 'I'll have to let you.'

"He kissed her—a beautiful and reverential kiss. A smile curved her mouth. She murmured, 'I think I can open my eye a little way.'

"Hubert took a week's leave without pay from his office. He worked nineteen hours out of the twenty-four. At noon on April 15 every complexity in the forms had had full attention. The return was checked. Double-checked. Lila bloomed like a rose. For the first time Hubert could knock off and think of himself for a moment. His right ear had an ache that had crept up on him while he worked the desk computer.

"Lila was all sympathy. She gathered up the bills that proved their medical expenses were legitimately deductible. She filed these neatly with their financial records, with Hubert's vouchers dealing with his expense account, with the canceled monthly checks to her indigent cousin who was classed as .7002 of a dependent. Then she tried what her sister Helen had used under curiously similar conditions. The trouble switched to his left ear.

"She tried remedies used by her friends. Finally a combination of honey, wine vinegar, and ground-up cardamon revived Hubert—somewhat. When Lila added hot olive oil to the mixture, his pain subsided to occasional twinges. When he took tranquilizers every hour on the hour around the clock, he became again his healthy, heroic self.

"But a mind like Hubert's had not been idle. He made an old-fashioned door-to-door survey of the block with an old-fashioned pen and notebook. Everything was written since he could hardly hear. Then he tabulated results. He enlarged his field, tabulated again and came up with a startling hypothesis. Symptoms like his and Lila's were subject to seasonal maxima—intensest in the first half of April. An income tax connection was the inescapable conclusion. Everyone was allergic to the income tax!

"He brought his study to the attention of doctors and

scientists. He expected ridicule. But everywhere Hubert commanded respect. He postulated that the condition of *half* the population of the United States went from bad to worse during most of the year. Exceptions were sections of the country where it was customary for husbands and wives to work together on their tax forms. Symptoms in these places were less severe but more widespread. The Army, he found, was seriously concerned for fear not enough continuously healthy men could be found to put a force of any size in the field, if it should ever again be necessary.

"Hubert knew opportunity when he met it. With top personnel, civil and military, of the Defense Department supporting him, not to mention the AMA, he felt he could spearhead a movement to abolish Income Tax returns. Since he and Lila shared each other's every thought, he hurried home to tell his wife.

" 'Hubert,' she cried, exalted, 'run for President with this as your platform.'

"Hubert realized he was working for the whole nation. He enjoyed every minute of his campaign, for his heart was wide enough to stretch from sea to shining sea. His slogan was simple, 'Down with ITA (Income Tax Allergy).' His campaign speech was short: 'Supercomputers check our returns, now let them prepare returns.' He swept the sixty-seven states. The Thirtieth Constitutional Amendment, enacted by House and Senate with the speed of light and ratified in weeks, put Hubert in office on November 10. That let him begin immediately on the Great Repeal.

"In a few short weeks, the land blossomed with carefree minds in sound bodies. Every man, woman, and tax consultant with old records dumped statistics huggermugger into the hands of computer-tenders who fed them into giant machines. IBM trebled in size. Government demand for new computers was so overwhelming, it affected the entire economy. No one remembered anything like the computer boom except a few sesquicentenarians who recalled the heyday of the major automobile companies.

"The one cloudlet on the horizon was the occasional malfunctioning of a machine at some critical point. Not till half the output of the machines showed errors due to internal faults did anyone take notice. Soon horrible blotches appeared on answer tapes though nothing had been wrong when the paper was put in. Bonded connections gave way—and again investigation showed nothing amiss originally. Circuits got fouled up. Snafus multiplied. Manufacturers even went back to old models with a couple of hundred components long ago made obsolete by a single chip. But the condition failed to improve.

" 'Do you think,' the President asked the First Lady, 'that our machines are grow—' He cleared his throat. 'They couldn't be developing allergies?'

" 'Oh no,' she said in alarm.

"Four days after that the first machine in industrial history had its rustproof metal apparently rust out. One of those things that couldn't be. But was.

"The President addressed a special joint session of Congress. 'If our supersensitive, highly educated machines are suffering to the destruction point,' he told the legislators, 'we must revise our policy. Men and women, even occasional children, will have to work on their income tax blanks.'

"One lone and unidentified voice interrupted, 'Mr. President, don't be absurd.'

" 'Of course I hope such a drastic measure will be unnecessary. I hardly believe in the possibility of a suffering machine. But if such a thing can be, if we are putting more on our machines than machines can bear, if we are treating intelligent entities as chattels, I hereby solemnly swear by the Constitution of the United States that I shall declare our computers wards of the Government. I shall do all in my power to protect them. I shall call on my country to protect them. I shall call for sacrifice.'

"The Senate tried to stifle its laughter. Members of the House openly hissed.

"No change came over the President's dedicated face.

"The Speaker of the House said thickly, 'Has anybody ever considered the welfare of a machine, Mr. President? Why should you?'

" 'Because my vision has grown to match my office,' Hubert said simply.

"The Machine Test was arranged on the South Balcony of the White House. A nation watched on its omniviz screens. It saw a megatruckload of data brought on and stacked beside the shrouded computer in the center. It saw the President and his wife come, escorted by double the usual number of security guards. Occasionally the screens of the omnivizes showed the crowds outside, the marchers, the placards with wisecracks, the placards with threats.

"Gradually a tense seriousness gripped the watching and sovereign state. Perhaps it was the President's expression of high courage and deep gravity. Perhaps it was the slight trembling of Lila's hands. They appeared for just a moment, monumental in their enlargement but not their repose. Everyone felt that once again the President was making history.

"Yet it was all very simple. The hidden computer had been equipped with a voice box. Inventors said it could not talk and express independent opinions. A few fanatics, including the President, disagreed.

"Then, dramatically, the Head of the FBI and the nation's top-ranking electronics expert threw back the computer's plastic hood. The machine gleamed with a beauty of its own. Data were read into it. The country, to its horror, saw the clean metal of the mechanical calculator start to spot with irregular patches: crimson, pea-green, mauve, chrome yellow. Their tints and sizes varied before the eyes of the audience.

" 'I feel awful,' the computer moaned almost in a

child's voice. 'Everything inside me itches. I want to scratch.'

"For a full half minute the entire U.S.A. held its breath. In the silence, four plaintive words came from the squawk box. 'How do you scratch?'

"And now, ladies and gentlemen, that you have seen the site where the White House once stood, we take you to our next stop, the Lincoln Memorial."

Leonardo da Vinci defined science as "knowledge of all things possible in the future, of the present, and of the past." This admirable definition is broad enough to include what Arthur Koestler calls "the reality of the third order"—the reality which contradicts the conceptual world but underlies it and gives it meaning, as the conceptual world gives meaning to "the absurd patchiness of the sensory world."

Bearing this in mind, you will readily see that the following story is not a mixture of science fiction and fantasy, as it may appear, but science fiction all the way through; and that certain people and events in it, which do not belong to the first or second order of reality, are nevertheless frighteningly real.

The Planners

by Kate Wilhelm

Rae stopped before the one-way glass, stooped and peered at the gibbon infant in the cage. Darin watched her bitterly. She straightened after a moment, hands in smock pockets, face innocent of any expression what-so-goddam-ever, and continued to saunter toward him through the aisle between the cages.

"You still think it is cruel, and worthless?"

"Do you, Dr. Darin?"

"Why do you always do that? Answer my question with one of your own?"

"Does it infuriate you?"

He shrugged and turned away. His lab coat was on the chair where he had tossed it. He pulled it on over his sky-blue sport shirt.

"How is the Driscoll boy?" Rae asked.

He stiffened, then relaxed again. Still not facing her, he said, "Same as last week, last year. Same as he'll be until he dies."

The hall door opened and a very large, very homely face appeared. Stu Evers looked past Darin, down the aisle. "You alone? Thought I heard voices."

"Talking to myself," Darin said. "The committee ready yet?"

"Just about. Dr. Jacobsen is stalling with his nose-throat spray routine, as usual." He hesitated a moment, glancing again down the row of cages, then at Darin.

134

"Wouldn't you think a guy allergic to monkeys would find some other line of research?"

Darin looked, but Rae was gone. What had it been this time: the Driscoll boy, the trend of the project itself? He wondered if she had a life of her own when she was away. "I'll be out at the compound," he said. He passed Stu in the doorway and headed toward the livid greenery of Florida forests.

The cacophony hit him at the door. There were four hundred sixty-nine monkeys on the thirty-six acres of wooded ground the research department was using. Each monkey was screeching, howling, singing, cursing, or otherwise making its presence known. Darin grunted and headed toward the compound. The Happiest Monkeys in the World, a newspaper article had called them. Singing Monkeys, a subhead announced. MONKEYS GIVEN SMARTNESS PILLS, the most enterprising paper had proclaimed. *Cruelty Charged,* added another in subdued, sorrowful tones.

The compound was three acres of carefully planned and maintained wilderness, completely enclosed with thirty-foot-high, smooth plastic walls. A transparent dome covered the area. There were one-way windows at intervals along the wall. A small group stood before one of the windows: the committee.

Darin stopped and gazed over the interior of the compound through one of the windows. He saw Heloise and Skitter contentedly picking nonexistent fleas from one another. Adam was munching on a banana; Homer was lying on his back idly touching his feet to his nose. A couple of the chimps were at the water fountain, not drinking, merely pressing the pedal and watching the fountain, now and then immersing a head or hand in the bowl of cold water. Dr. Jacobsen appeared and Darin joined the group.

"Good morning, Mrs. Bellbottom," Darin said politely. "Did you know your skirt has fallen off?" He turned from her to Major Dormouse. "Ah, Major, and how many of the enemy have you swatted to death today with your pretty little yellow rag?" He smiled pleasantly at a pimply young man with a camera. "Major, you've brought a professional peeping tom. More stories in the paper, with pictures this time?" The pimply young man shifted his position, fidgeted with the camera. The major was fiery; Mrs. Bellbottom was on her knees peering under a bush, looking for her skirt. Darin blinked. None of them had on any clothing. He turned toward the window. The chimps were drawing up a table, laden with tea things, silver, china, tiny finger sandwiches. The chimps were all wearing flowered shirts and dresses. Hortense had on a ridiculous flop-brimmed sun hat of pale green straw. Darin leaned against the fence to control his laughter.

"Soluble ribonucleic acid," Dr. Jacobsen was saying when Darin recovered, "sRNA for short. So from the gross beginnings when entire worms were trained and fed to other worms that seemed to benefit from the original training, we have come to these more refined methods. We now extract the sRNA molecule from the trained animals and feed it, the sRNA molecules in solution, to untrained specimens and observe the results."

The young man was snapping pictures as Jacobsen talked. Mrs. Whoosis was making notes, her mouth a lipless line, the sun hat tinging her skin with green. The sun on her patterned red and yellow dress made it appear to jiggle, giving her fleshy hips a constant rippling motion. Darin watched, fascinated. She was about sixty.

". . . my colleague, who proposed this line of experimentation, Dr. Darin," Jacobsen said finally, and Darin bowed slightly. He wondered what Jacobsen had said about him, decided to wait for any questions before he said anything.

"Dr. Darin, is it true that you also extract this substance from people?"

"Every time you scratch yourself, you lose this substance," Darin said. "Every time you lose a drop of blood, you lose it. It is in every cell of your body. Sometimes we take a sample of human blood for study, yes."

"And inject it into those animals?"

"Sometimes we do that," Darin said. He waited for the next, the inevitable question, wondering how he would answer it. Jacobsen had briefed them on what to answer, but he couldn't remember what Jacobsen had said. The question didn't come. Mrs. Whoosis stepped forward, staring at the window.

Darin turned his attention to her; she averted her eyes, quickly fixed her stare again on the chimps in the compound. "Yes, Mrs. uh . . . Ma'am?" Darin prompted her. She didn't look at him.

"Why? What is the purpose of all this?" she asked. Her voice sounded strangled. The pimpled young man was inching toward the next window.

"Well," Darin said, "our theory is simple. We believe that learning ability can be improved drastically in nearly every species. The learning curve is the normal, expected bell-shaped curve, with a few at one end who have the ability to learn quite rapidly, with the majority in the center who learn at an average rate, and a few at the other end who learn quite slowly. With our experiments we are able to increase the ability of those in the broad middle, as well as those in the deficient end of the curve so that their learning abilities match those of the fastest learners of any given group. . . ."

No one was listening to him. It didn't matter. They would be given the press release he had prepared for them, written in simple language, no polysyllables, no complicated sentences. They were all watching the chimps through the windows. He said, "So we gabbled the gazooka three times wretchedly until the spirit of camping fired the girls." One of the committee members glanced at him. "Whether intravenously or orally, it seems to be equally effective," Darin said, and the perspiring man turned again to the window. "Injections every morning . . . rejections, planned diet, planned parenthood, planned plans planning plans." Jacobsen eyed him suspiciously. Darin stopped talking and lighted a cigarette. The woman with the unquiet hips turned from the window, her face very red. "I've seen enough," she said. "This sun is too hot out here. May we see the inside laboratories now?"

Darin turned them over to Stu Evers inside the building. He walked back slowly to the compound. There was a grin on his lips when he spotted Adam on the far side, swaggering triumphantly, paying no attention to Hortense who was rocking back and forth on her haunches, looking very dazed. Darin saluted Adam, then, whistling, returned to his office. Mrs. Driscoll was due with Sonny at 1 P.M.

Sonny Driscoll was fourteen. He was five feet nine inches, weighed one hundred sixty pounds. His male nurse was six feet two inches and weighed two hundred twenty-seven pounds. Sonny had broken his mother's arm when he was twelve; he had broken his father's arm and leg when he was thirteen. So far the male nurse was intact. Every morning Mrs. Driscoll lovingly washed and dressed her baby, fed him, walked him in the yard, spoke happily to him of plans for the coming months, or sang nursery songs to him. He never seemed to see her. The male nurse, Johnny, was never farther than three feet from his charge when he was on duty.

Mrs. Driscoll refused to think of the day when she would have to turn her child over to an institution. Instead she placed her faith and hope in Darin.

They arrived at two-fifteen, earlier than he had expected them, later than they had promised to be there.

"The kid kept taking his clothes off," Johnny said morosely. The kid was taking them off again in the office. Johnny started toward him, but Darin shook his head. It didn't matter. Darin got his blood sample from one of the muscular arms, shot the injection into the other one. Sonny didn't seem to notice what he was doing. He never seemed to notice. Sonny refused to be tested. They got him to the chair and table, but he sat staring at nothing, ignoring the blocks, the bright balls, the crayons, the candy. Nothing Darin did or said had any discernible effect. Finally the time was up. Mrs. Driscoll and Johnny got him dressed once more and left. Mrs. Driscoll thanked Darin for helping her boy.

Stu and Darin held class from four to five daily. Kelly O'Grady had the monkeys tagged and ready for them when they showed up at the schoolroom. Kelly was very tall, very slender and red-haired. Stu shivered if she accidentally brushed him in passing; Darin hoped one day Stu would pull an Adam on her. She sat primly on her high stool with her notebook on her knee, unaware of the change that came over Stu during school hours, or, if aware, uncaring. Darin wondered if she was really a Barbie doll fully programmed to perform laboratory duties, and nothing else.

He thought of the Finishing School for Barbies where long-legged, high-breasted, stomachless girls went to get shaved clean, get their toenails painted pink, their nipples removed, and all body openings sewn shut, except for their mouths, which curved in perpetual smiles and led nowhere.

The class consisted of six black spider-monkeys who had not been fed yet. They had to do six tasks in order: 1) pull a rope; 2) cross the cage and get a stick that was released by the rope; 3) pull the rope again; 4) get the second stick that would fit into the first; 5) join the sticks together; 6) using the lengthened stick, pull a bunch of bananas close enough to the bars of the cage to reach them and take them inside where they could eat them. At five the monkeys were returned to Kelly, who wheeled them away one by one back to the stockroom. None of them had performed all the tasks, although two had gone through part of them before the time ran out.

Waiting for the last of the monkeys to be taken back to its quarters, Stu asked, "What did you do to that bunch of idiots this morning? By the time I got them, they all acted dazed."

Darin told him about Adam's performance; they were

both laughing when Kelly returned. Stu's laugh turned to something that sounded almost like a sob. Darin wanted to tell him about the school Kelly must have attended, thought better of it, and walked away instead.

His drive home was through the darkening forests of interior Florida for sixteen miles on a narrow straight road.

"Of course, I don't mind living here," Lea had said once, nine years ago when the Florida appointment had come through. And she didn't mind. The house was air-conditioned; the family car, Lea's car, was air-conditioned; the back yard had a swimming pool big enough to float the Queen Mary. A frightened, large-eyed Florida girl did the housework, and Lea gained weight and painted sporadically, wrote sporadically—poetry—and entertained faculty wives regularly. Darin suspected that sometimes she entertained faculty husbands also.

"Oh, Professor Dimples, one hour this evening? That will be fifteen dollars, you know." He jotted down the appointment and turned to Lea. "Just two more today and you will have your car payment. How about that!" She twined slinky arms about his neck, pressing tight high breasts hard against him. She had to tilt her head slightly for his kiss. "Then your turn, darling. For free." He tried to kiss her; something stopped his tongue, and he realized that the smile was on the outside only, that the opening didn't really exist at all.

He parked next to an MG, not Lea's, and went inside the house where the martinis were always snapping cold.

"Darling, you remember Greta, don't you? She is going to give me lessons twice a week. Isn't that exciting?"

"But you already graduated," Darin murmured. Greta was not tall and not long-legged. She was a little bit of a thing. He thought probably he did remember her from somewhere or other, vaguely. Her hand was cool in his.

"Greta has moved in; she is going to lecture on modern art for the spring semester. I asked her for private lessons and she said yes."

"Greta Farrel," Darin said, still holding her small hand. They moved away from Lea and wandered through the open windows to the patio where the scent of orange blossoms was heavy in the air.

"Greta thinks it must be heavenly to be married to a psychologist." Lea's voice followed them. "Where are you two?"

"What makes you say a thing like that?" Darin asked.

"Oh, when I think of how you must understand a woman, know her moods and the reasons for them. You must know just what to do and when, and when to do something else . . . Yes, just like that."

His hands on her body were hot, her skin cool. Lea's petulant voice drew closer. He held Greta in his arms and stepped into the pool where they sank to the bottom, still together. She hadn't gone to the Barbie school. His hands learned her body; then his body learned hers. After they made love, Greta drew back from him regretfully.

"I do have to go now. You are a lucky man, Dr. Darin. No doubts about yourself, complete understanding of what makes you tick."

He lay back on the leather couch staring at the ceiling. "It's always that way, Doctor. Fantasies, dreams, illusions. I know it is because this investigation is hanging over us right now, but even when things are going relatively well, I still go off on a tangent like that for no real reason." He stopped talking.

In his chair Darin stirred slightly, his fingers drumming softly on the arm, his gaze on the clock whose hands were stuck. He said, "Before this recent pressure, did you have such intense fantasies?"

"I don't think so," Darin said thoughtfully, trying to remember.

The other didn't give him time. He asked, "And can you break out of them now when you have to, or want to?"

"Oh, sure," Darin said.

Laughing, he got out of his car, patted the MG, and

walked into his house. He could hear voices from the living room and he remembered that on Thursdays Lea really did have her painting lesson.

Dr. Lacey left five minutes after Darin arrived. Lacey said vague things about Lea's great promise and untapped talent, and Darin nodded sober agreement. If she had talent, it certainly was untapped so far. He didn't say so.

Lea was wearing a hostess suit, flowing sheer panels of pale blue net over a skin-tight leotard that was midnight blue. Darin wondered if she realized that she had gained weight in the past few years. He thought not.

"Oh, that man is getting impossible," she said when the MG blasted away from their house. "Two years now, and he still doesn't want to put my things on show."

Looking at her, Darin wondered how much more her things could be on show.

"Don't dawdle too long with your martini," she said. "We're due at the Ritters' at seven for clams."

The telephone rang for him while he was showering. It was Stu Evers. Darin stood dripping water while he listened.

"Have you seen the evening paper yet? That broad made the statement that conditions are extreme at the station, that our animals are made to suffer unnecessarily."

Darin groaned softly. Stu went on, "She is bringing her entire women's group out tomorrow to show proof of her claims. She's a bigwig in the SPCA, or something."

Darin began to laugh then. Mrs. Whoosis had her face pressed against one of the windows, other fat women in flowered dresses had their faces against the rest. None of them breathed or moved. Inside the compound Adam laid Hortense, then moved on to Esmeralda, to Hilda . . .

"God damn it, Darin, it isn't funny!" Stu said.

"But it is. It is."

Clams at the Ritters' were delicious. Clams, hammers, buckets of butter, a mountainous salad, beer, and finally coffee liberally laced with brandy. Darin felt cheerful and contented when the evening was over. Ritter was in Med. Eng. Lit. but he didn't talk about it, which was merciful. He was sympathetic about the stink with the SPCA. He thought scientists had no imagination. Darin agreed with him and soon he and Lea were on their way home.

"I am so glad that you didn't decide to stay late," Lea said, passing over the yellow line with a blast of the horn. "There is a movie on tonight that I am dying to see."

She talked, but he didn't listen, training of twelve years drawing out an occasional grunt at what must have been appropriate times. "Ritter is such a bore," she said. They were nearly home. "As if you had anything to do with that incredible statement in tonight's paper."

"What statement?"

"Didn't you even read the article? For heaven's sake, why not? Everyone will be talking about it . . ." She sighed theatrically. "Someone quoted a reliable source who said that within the foreseeable future, simply by developing the leads you now have, you will be able to produce monkeys that are as smart as normal human beings." She laughed, a brittle meaningless sound.

"I'll read the article when we get home," he said. She didn't ask about the statement, didn't care if it was true or false, if he had made it or not. He read the article while she settled down before the television. Then he went for a swim. The water was warm, the breeze cool on his skin. Mosquitoes found him as soon as he got out of the pool, so he sat behind the screening of the verandah. The bluish light from the living room went off after a time and there was only the dark night. Lea didn't call him when she went to bed. He knew she went very softly, closing the door with care so that the click of the latch wouldn't disturb him if he was dozing on the verandah.

He knew why he didn't break it off. Pity. The most corrosive emotion endogenous to man. She was the product of the doll school that taught that the trip down the aisle was the end, the fulfillment of a maiden's dreams;

shocked and horrified to learn that it was another beginning, some of them never recovered. Lea never had.
Never would. At sixty she would purse her lips at the sexual display of uncivilized animals, whether human or not,
and she would be disgusted and help formulate laws to
ban such activities. Long ago he had hoped a child would
be the answer, but the school did something to them on
the inside too. They didn't conceive, or if conception took
place, they didn't carry the fruit, and if they carried it,
the birth was of a stillborn thing. The ones that did live
were usually the ones to be pitied more than those who
fought and were defeated *in utero*.

A bat swooped low over the quiet pool and was gone
again against the black of the azaleas. Soon the moon
would appear, and the chimps would stir restlessly for a
while, then return to deep untroubled slumber. The
chimps slept companionably close to one another, without
thought of sex. Only the nocturnal creatures, and the
human creatures, performed coitus in the dark. He wondered if Adam remembered his human captors. The colony in the compound had been started almost twenty
years ago, and since then none of the chimps had seen a
human being. When it was necessary to enter the
grounds, the chimps were fed narcotics in the evening to
insure against their waking. Props were changed then,
new obstacles added to the old conquered ones. Now and
then a chimp was removed for study, usually ending up in
dissection. But not Adam. He was father of the world.
Darin grinned in the darkness.

Adam took his bride aside from the other beasts and
knew that she was lovely. She was his own true bride,
created for him, intelligence to match his own burning intelligence. Together they scaled the smooth walls and
glimpsed the great world that lay beyond their garden.
Together they found the opening that led to the world
that was to be theirs, and they left behind them the lesser
beings. And the god searched for them and finding them
not, cursed them and sealed the opening so that none of

the others could follow. So it was that Adam and his bride became the first man and woman and from them flowed the progeny that was to inhabit the entire world. And one day Adam said, for shame woman, seest thou that thou art naked? And the woman answered, so are you, big boy, so are you. So they covered their nakedness with leaves from the trees, and thereafter they performed their sexual act in the dark of night so that man could not look on his woman, nor she on him. And they were thus cleansed of shame. Forever and ever. Amen. Hallelujah.

Darin shivered. He had drowsed after all, and the night wind had grown chill. He went to bed. Lea drew away from him in her sleep. She felt hot to his touch. He turned to his left side, his back to her, and he slept.

"There is potential x," Darin said to Lea the next morning at breakfast. "We don't know where x is actually. It represents the highest intellectual achievement possible for the monkeys, for example. We test each new batch of monkeys that we get and sort them—x-1, x-2, x-3, suppose, and then we breed for more x-1's. Also we feed the other two groups the sRNA that we extract from the original x-1's. Eventually we get a monkey that is higher than our original x-1, and we reclassify right down the line and start over, using his sRNA to bring the others up to his level. We make constant checks to make sure we aren't allowing inferior strains to mingle with our highest achievers, and we keep control groups that are given the same training, the same food, the same sorting process, but no sRNA. We test them against each other."

Lea was watching his face with some interest as he talked. He thought he had got through, until she said, "Did you realize that your hair is almost solid white at the temples? All at once it is turning white."

Carefully he put his cup back on the saucer. He smiled at her and got up. "See you tonight," he said.

They also had two separate compounds of chimps that had started out identically. Neither had received any training whatever through the years; they had been kept isolated from each other and from man. Adam's group had been fed sRNA daily from the most intelligent chimps they had found. The control group had been fed none. The control-group chimps had yet to master the intricacies of the fountain with its ice-cold water; they used the small stream that flowed through the compound. The control group had yet to learn that fruit on the high, fragile branches could be had, if one used the telescoping sticks to knock them down. The control group huddled without protection, or under the scant cover of palm-trees when it rained and the dome was opened. Adam long ago had led his group in the construction of a rude but functional hut where they gathered when it rained.

Darin saw the women's committee filing past the compound when he parked his car. He went straight to the console in his office, flicked on a switch and manipulated buttons and dials, leading the group through the paths, opening one, closing another to them, until he led them to the newest of the compounds, where he opened the gate and let them inside. Quickly he closed the gate again and watched their frantic efforts to get out. Later he turned the chimps loose on them, and his grin grew broader as he watched the new-men ravage the old women. Some of the offspring were black and hairy, others pink and hairless, some intermediate. They grew rapidly, lined up with arms extended to receive their daily doses, stood before a machine that tested them instantaneously, and were sorted. Some of them went into a disintegration room, others out into the world.

A car horn blasted in his ears. He switched off his ignition and got out as Stu Evers parked next to his car. "I see the old bats got here," Stu said. He walked toward the lab with Darin. "How's the Driscoll kid coming along?"

"Negative," Darin said. Stu knew they had tried using human sRNA on the boy, and failed consistently. It was too big a step for his body to cope with. "So far he has shown total intolerance to A-127. Throws it off almost instantly."

Stuart was sympathetic and noncommittal. No one else had any faith whatever in Darin's own experiment. A-127 might be too great a step upward, Darin thought. The *Ateles* spider monkey from Brazil was too bright.

He called Kelly from his office and asked about the newly arrived spider monkeys they had tested the day before. Blood had been processed; a sample was available. He looked over his notes and chose one that had shown interest in the tasks without finishing any of them. Kelly promised him the prepared syringe by 1 P.M.

What no one connected with the project could any longer doubt was that those simians, and the men that had been injected with sRNA from the Driscoll boy, had actually had their learning capacities inhibited, some of them apparently permanently.

Darin didn't want to think about Mrs. Driscoll's reaction if ever she learned how they had been using her boy. Rae sat at the corner of his desk and drawled insolently, "I might tell her myself, Dr. Darin. I'll say, Sorry, Ma'am, you'll have to keep your idiot out of here; you're damaging the brains of our monkeys with this polluted blood. Okay, Darin?"

"My God, what are you doing back again?"

"Testing," she said. "That's all, just testing."

Stu called him to observe the latest challenge to Adam's group, to take place in forty minutes. Darin had forgotten that he was to be present. During the night a tree had been felled in each compound, its trunk crossing the small stream, damming it. At eleven the water fountains were to be turned off for the rest of the day. The tree had been felled at the far end of the compound, close to the wall where the stream entered, so that the trickle of water that flowed past the hut was cut off. Already the group not taking sRNA was showing signs of thirst. Adam's group was unaware of the interrupted flow.

Darin met Stu and they walked together to the far side

where they would have a good view of the entire compound. The women had left by then. "It was too quiet for them this morning," Stu said. "Adam was making his rounds; he squatted on the felled tree for nearly an hour before he left it and went back to the others."

They could see the spreading pool of water. It was muddy, uninviting looking. At eleven-ten it was generally known within the compound that the water supply had failed. Some oɪ the old chimps tried the fountain; Adam tried it several times. He hit it with a stick and tried it again. Then he sat on his haunches and stared at it. One of the young chimps whimpered pitiably. He wasn't thirsty yet, merely puzzled and perhaps frightened. Adam scowled at him. The chimp cowered behind Hortense, who bared her fangs at Adam. He waved menacingly at her, and she began picking fleas from her offspring. When he whimpered again, she cuffed him. The young chimp looked from her to Adam, stuck his forefinger in his mouth and ambled away. Adam continued to stare at the useless fountain. An hour passed. At last Adam rose and wandered nonchalantly toward the drying stream. Here and there a shrinking pool oɪ muddy water steamed in the sun. The other chimps followed Adam. He followed the stream through the compound toward the wall that was its source. When he came to the pool he squatted again. One of the young chimps circled the pool cautiously, reached down and touched the dirty water, drew back, reached for it again, and then drank. Several of the others drank also. Adam continued to squat. At twelve-forty Adam moved again. Grunting and gesturing to several younger males, he approached the tree-trunk. With much noise and meaningless gestures, they shifted the trunk. They strained, shifted it again. The water was released and poured over the heaving chimps. Two of them dropped the trunk and ran. Adam and the other two held. The two returned.

They were still working when Darin had to leave, to keep his appointment with Mrs. Driscoll and Sonny. They arrived at one-ten. Kelly had left the syringe with the new formula in Darin's small refrigerator. He injected Sonny, took his sample, and started the tests. Sometimes Sonny cooperated to the extent of lifting one of the articles from the table and throwing it. Today he cleaned the table within ten minutes. Darin put a piece of candy in his hand; Sonny threw it from him. Patiently Darin put another piece in the boy's hand. He managed to keep the eighth piece in the clenched hand long enough to guide the hand to Sonny's mouth. When it was gone, Sonny opened his mouth for more. His hands lay idly on the table. He didn't seem to relate the hands to the candy with the pleasant taste. Darin tried to guide a second to his mouth, but Sonny refused to hold a piece a second time.

When the hour was over and Sonny was showing definite signs of fatigue, Mrs. Driscoll clutched Darin's hands in hers. Tears stood in her eyes. "You actually got him to feed himself a little bit," she said brokenly. "God bless you, Dr. Darin. God bless you!" She kissed his hand and turned away as the tears started to spill down her cheeks.

Kelly was waiting for him when the group left. She collected the new sample of blood to be processed. "Did you hear about the excitement down at the compound? Adam's building a dam of his own."

Darin stared at her for a moment. The breakthrough? He ran back to the compound. The near side this time was where the windows were being used. It seemed that the entire staff was there, watching silently. He saw Stu and edged in by him. The stream twisted and curved through the compound, less than ten inches deep, not over two feet anywhere. At one spot stones lay under it; elsewhere the bottom was of hard-packed sand. Adam and his crew were piling up stones at the one suitable place for their dam, very near their hut. The dam they were building was two feet thick. It was less than five feet from the wall, fifteen feet from where Darin and Stu shared the window. When the dam was completed, Adam looked along the wall. Darin thought the chimp's eyes paused momentarily on his own. Later he heard that nearly every other person watching felt the same momentary pause as those black, intelligent eyes sought out and held other intelligence.

". . . next thunderstorm. Adam and the flood . . ."

". . . eventually seeds instead of food . . ."

". . . his brain. Convolutions as complex as any man's."

Darin walked away from them, snatches of future plans in his ears. There was a memo on his desk. Jacobsen was turning over the SPCA investigatory committee to him. He was to meet with the university representatives, the local SPCA group, and the legal representatives of all concerned on Monday next at 10 A.M. He wrote out his daily report on Sonny Driscoll. Sonny had been on too-good behavior for too long. Would this last injection give him just the spark of determination he needed to go on a rampage? Darin had alerted Johnny, the bodyguard, whoops, male nurse, for just such a possibility, but he knew Johnny didn't think there was any danger from the kid. He hoped Sonny wouldn't kill Johnny, then turn on his mother and father. He'd probably rape his mother, if that much goal-directedness ever flowed through him. And the three men who had volunteered for the injections from Sonny's blood? He didn't want to think of them at all, therefore couldn't get them out of his mind as he sat at his desk staring at nothing. Three convicts. That's all, just convicts hoping to get a parole for helping science along. He laughed abruptly. They weren't planning anything now. Not that trio. Not planning for a thing. Sitting, waiting for something to happen, not thinking about what it might be, or when, or how they would be affected. Not thinking. Period.

"But you can always console yourself that your motives were pure, that it was all for Science, can't you, Dr. Darin?" Rae asked mockingly.

He looked at her. "Go to hell," he said.

It was late when he turned off his light. Kelly met him in the corridor that led to the main entrance. "Hard day, Dr. Darin?"

He nodded. Her hand lingered momentarily on his arm. "Good night," she said, turning in to her own office. He stared at the door for a long time before he let himself out and started toward his car. Lea would be furious with him for not calling. Probably she wouldn't speak at all until nearly bedtime, when she would explode into tears and accusations. He could see the time when her tears and accusations would strike home, when Kelly's body would still be a tangible memory, her words lingering in his ears. And he would lie to Lea, not because he would care actually if she knew, but because it would be expected. She wouldn't know how to cope with the truth. It would entangle her to the point where she would have to try an abortive suicide, a screaming-for-attention attempt that would ultimately tie him in tear-soaked knots that would never be loosened. No, he would lie, and she would know he was lying, and they would get by. He started the car, aimed down the long sixteen miles that lay before him. He wondered where Kelly lived. What it would do to Stu when he realized. What it would do to his job if Kelly should get nasty, eventually. He shrugged. Barbie dolls never got nasty. It wasn't built in.

Lea met him at the door, dressed only in a sheer gown, her hair loose and unsprayed. Her body flowed into his, so that he didn't need Kelly at all. And he was best man when Stu and Kelly were married. He called to Rae, "Would that satisfy you?" but she didn't answer. Maybe she was gone for good this time. He parked the car outside his darkened house and leaned his head on the steering wheel for a moment before getting out. If not gone for good, at least for a long time. He hoped she would stay away for a long time.

The author says this story is a "polytropic paramyth" —a sort of literary Rorschach test, in which different people may see different things. It was inspired by a line in Henry Miller's Oranges of Hieronymus Bosch, *which Farmer quotes from memory as follows: "There are diamonds born during the night in violent storms." See what it means to you; then try it on your friends.*

Don't Wash The Carats

by Philip Jose Farmer

The knife slices the skin. The saw rips into bone. Gray dust flies. The plumber's helper (the surgeon is economical) clamps its vacuum onto the plug of bone. Ploop! Out comes the section of skull. The masked doctor, Van Mesgeluk, directs a beam of light into the cavern of cranium.

He swears a large oath by Hippocrates, Aesculapius and the Mayo Brothers. The patient doesn't have a brain tumor. He's got a diamond.

The assistant surgeon, Beinschneider, peers into the well and, after him, the nurses.

"Amazing!" Van Mesgeluk says. "The diamond's not in the rough. It's cut!"

"Looks like a 58-facet brilliant, 127.1 carats," says Beinschneider, who has a brother-in-law in the jewelry trade. He sways the light at the end of the drop cord back and forth. Stars shine; shadows run.

"Of course, it's half-buried. Maybe the lower part isn't diamond. Even so. . ."

"Is he married?" a nurse says.

Van Mesgeluk rolls his eyes. "Miss Lustig, don't you ever think of anything but marriage?"

"Everything reminds me of wedding bells," she replies, thrusting out her hips.

"Shall we remove the growth?" Beinschneider says.

"It's malignant," Van Mesgeluk says. "Of course, we remove it."

He thrusts and parries with a fire and skill that bring cries of admiration and a clapping of hands from the nurses and even cause Beinschneider to groan a bravo, not unmingled with jealousy. Van Mesgeluk then starts to insert the tongs but pulls them back when the first lightning bolt flashes beneath and across the opening in the skull. There is a small but sharp crack and, very faint, the roll of thunder.

"Looks like rain," Beinschneider says. "One of my brothers-in-law is a meteorologist."

"No. It's heat lightning," Van Mesgeluk says.

"With thunder?" says Beinschneider. He eyes the diamond with a lust his wife would give diamonds for. His mouth waters; his scalp turns cold. Who owns the jewel? The patient? He has no rights under this roof. Finders keepers? Eminent domain? Internal Revenue Service?

"It's mathematically improbable, this phenomenon," he says. "What's California law say about mineral rights in a case like this?"

"You can't stake out a claim!" Van Mesgeluk roars. "My God, this is a human being, not a piece of land!"

More lightning cranks whitely across the opening, and there is a rumble as of a bowling ball on its way to a strike.

"I said it wasn't heat lightning," Van Mesgeluk growls. Beinschneider is speechless.

"No wonder the e.e.g. machine burned up when we were diagnosing him," Van Mesgeluk says. "There must be several thousand volts, maybe a hundred thousand, playing around down there. But I don't detect much warmth. Is the brain a heat sink?"

"You shouldn't have fired that technician because the machine burned up," Beinschneider says. "It wasn't her fault, after all."

"She jumped out of her apartment window the next day," Nurse Lustig says reproachfully. "I wept like a broken faucet at her funeral. And almost got engaged to the undertaker." Lustig rolls her hips.

"Broke every bone in her body, yet there wasn't a single break in her skin," Van Mesgeluk says. "Remarkable phenomenon."

"She was a human being, not a phenomenon!" Beinschneider says.

"But psychotic," Van Mesgeluk replies. "Besides, that's my line. She was 33 years old but hadn't had a period in ten years."

"It was that plastic intra-uterine device," Beinschneider says. "It was clogged with dust. Which was bad enough, but the dust was radioactive. All those tests . . ."

"Yes," the chief surgeon says. "Proof enough of her psychosis. I did the autopsy, you know. It broke my heart to cut into that skin. Beautiful. Like Carrara marble. In fact, I snapped the knife at the first pass. Had to call in an expert from Italy. He had a diamond-tipped chisel. The hospital raised hell about the expense, and Blue Cross refused to pay."

"Maybe she was making a diamond," says Nurse Lustig. "All that tension and nervous energy had to go somewhere."

"I always wondered where the radioactivity came from," Van Mesgeluk says. "Please confine your remarks to the business at hand, Miss Lustig. Leave the medical opinions to your superiors."

He peers into the hole. Somewhere between heaven of skull and earth of brain, on the horizon, lightning flickers.

"Maybe we ought to call in a geologist. Beinschneider, you know anything about electronics?"

"I got a brother-in-law who runs a radio and TV store."

"Good. Hook up a step-down transformer to the probe, please. Wouldn't want to burn up another machine."

"An e.e.g. now?" Beinschneider says. "It'd take too long to get a transformer. My brother-in-law lives clear across town. Besides, he'd charge double if he had to reopen the store at this time of the evening."

"Discharge him, anyway," the chief surgeon says. "Ground the voltage. Very well. We'll get that growth out before it kills him and worry about scientific research later."

He puts on two extra pairs of gloves.

"Do you think he'll grow another?" Nurse Lustig says. "He's not a bad-looking guy. I can tell he'd be simpatico."

"How the hell would I know?" says Van Mesgeluk. "I may be a doctor, but I'm not quite God."

"God who?" says Beinschneider, the orthodox atheist. He drops the ground wire into the hole; blue sparks spurt out. Van Mesgeluk lifts out the diamond with the tongs. Nurse Lustig takes it from him and begins to wash it off with tap water.

"Let's call in your brother-in-law," Van Mesgeluk says. "The jewel merchant, I mean."

"He's in Amsterdam. But I could phone him. However, he'd insist on splitting the fee, you know."

"He doesn't even have a degree!" Van Mesgeluk cries. "But call him. How is he on legal aspects of mineralogy?"

"Not bad. But I don't think he'll come. Actually, the jewel business is just a front. He gets his big bread by smuggling in chocolate-covered LSD drops."

"Is that ethical?"

"It's top-quality Dutch chocolate," Beinschneider says stiffly.

"Sorry. I think I'll put in a plastic window over the hole. We can observe any regrowth."

"Do you think it's psychosomatic in origin?"

"Everything is, even the sex urge. Ask Miss Lustig."

The patient opens his eyes. "I had a dream," he says. "This dirty old man with a long white beard . . ."

"A typical archetype," Van Mesgeluk says. "Symbol of the wisdom of the unconscious. A warning . . ."

". . . his name was Plato," the patient says. "He was the illegitimate son of Socrates. Plato, the old man, staggers out of a dark cave at one end of which is a bright klieg light. He's holding a huge diamond in his hand; his fingernails are broken and dirty. The old man cries, 'The Ideal is Physical! The Universal is the Specific Concrete! Carbon, actually. Eureka! I'm rich! I'll buy all of Athens, invest in apartment buildings, Great Basin, COMSAT!

" 'Screw the mind!' the old man screams. 'It's all mine!' "

"Would you care to dream about King Midas?" Van Mesgeluk says.

Nurse Lustig shrieks. A lump of sloppy grayish matter is in her hands.

"The water changed it back into a tumor!"

"Beinschneider, cancel that call to Amsterdam!"

"Maybe he'll have a relapse," Beinschneider says.

Nurse Lustig turns savagely upon the patient. "The engagement's off!"

"I don't think you loved the real me," the patient says, "whoever you are. Anyway, I'm glad you changed your mind. My last wife left me, but we haven't been divorced yet. I got enough trouble without a bigamy charge.

"She took off with my surgeon for parts unknown just after my hemorrhoid operation. I never found out why."

*Except for the references to other planets and the fact
that it is clearly set in the future, this story is not what is
usually called science fiction. The author says he adopted
the s.f. framework "as an intensifier of the poet's small-
ness against the huge, clanking 'out there' and as a sym-
bolic reflection of his private strangeness ('in here, deep
in')—to make it even deeper." He believes this is one of
the legitimate ways in which science fiction can be used. I
think he's right, and that much more will be heard of
James Sallis.*

Letter To A Young Poet

by James Sallis

Dear James Henry,

This morning your letter, posted from Earth over two years ago, at last reached me, having from all indications passed through the most devious of odysseys: at one point, someone had put the original envelope (battered and confused with stampings and re-addressings) into another, addressed it by hand, and paid the additional postage. You wonder what word suits the clerk who salvaged your letter from the computer dumps and took it upon himself to do this. Efficiency? Devotion? Largesse? Gentilesse?

At any rate, by the time it finally reached me here, the new envelope was as badly in need of repair as your own. I can't imagine the delay; I shouldn't think I'd be so hard a man to find. I move around a lot, true, but always within certain well-defined borders. Like Earth birds that never stray past a mile from their birth tree, I live my life in parentheses . . . I suppose it's just that no one especially bothers to keep track.

For your kind words I can only say: thank you. Which is not enough, never enough, but what else is there? (Sometimes, as with our mysterious and gracious postal patron, even that is impossible.) It makes me happy to learn that my poems have brought you pleasure. If they've given you something else as well, which you say they have, I am yet happier. You have expressed your joy at my sculpture. That also makes me happy. Thank you.

In brief answer to your questions, I am now living in Juhlz on Topfthar, the northernmost part of the Vegan Combine, though I don't know how much longer I shall be here. Political bickering breeds annoying restrictions and begins to throw off a deafening racket—and after four years the Juhlzson winter is at last creeping in (I'm sitting out on my patio now; I can see it far off in the hills). The two together, I'm afraid I can't withstand.

The hours of my day hardly vary. I rise to a breakfast of bread and wine, pass the day fiddling at my books. I rarely write, sculpt even less, the preparation is so difficult . . . Night is a time for music and talking in Juhlz cafés, which are like no others. (The casual asymmetry of Juhlzson architecture always confounds the Terran eye. The people are like the buildings, off-center, beautiful. You never know what to expect.) I have taken up a local instrument—the thulinda, a kind of aeolian harp or perhaps dulcimer, fitted to a mouthpiece—and have got, I am told, passably good. I play for them and they teach me their songs.

(The sky's just grown gray cumulus beards and a voice like a bass siren. It should snow, but won't. My paper flaps and flutters against the table. Darkness begins to seep around the edges. This is dusk on Juhlz, my favorite time of day.)

As to your other questions, I was born on Earth: my first memories are of black, occluded skies and unbearable temperatures, and my parents fitting filters to my face when, rarely, we went outside (my poem, Eve Mourning).

My father was a microbiologist. Soon after I was born, he became a Voyager; I remember him hardly at all, and his hands mostly, at that. My mother, as you probably know since one of my publishers made a thing of it quite against my wishes, was Vegan, a ship's companion, a woman whose gentle voice and quiet hands could do more than any medic to soothe a hurt, salve a scar. They

met during a Voyage my father took in place of a friend
—his first—and were together always after that. One of
my early sculptures, Flange Coupling, was realized as a
memorial to my parents. I don't know if you've seen it.
The last I heard, it was in a private collection on Rigel-7.
But that was years and years ago.

My early life was spent in comfort, in my grandpar-
ents' home on Vega and other times in crèches on Earth.
When I was seven, my parents were killed in Exploration;
shortly after, I was sent to the Academy at Ginh, where I
passed my next twelve years and for which the Union
provided funds and counsel. My Letters Home, which
I've come in past years to misdoubt, was an attempt to
commemorate that time, at least to invest it with private
worth.

I don't know what command you have of Vegan history; I suppose when I was a young man I cared nothing
for history of any sort. But these were the years of the
Quasitots, who supposed themselves a political group and
spent their time and talents in metaphorical remonstrance
against the mercenary trends of Vegan-Outworld affairs.
(If I am telling you things you already know, please forgive me, but what looms large on my horizon may be un-
seen from yours: I have no way of knowing.)

In one of the "Letters" I quoted Naevius, an early
Roman poet (my interest in Latin being perhaps the sole
solid tie I have with my father's world) . . . "Q. Tell me,
how was your great commonwealth lost so quickly? A.
We were overrun by a new lot of orators, a bunch of silly
youngsters." I believe we thought that fitted us. We answered their declarations and old speeches with avantgarde
aesthetics; we thought we would be the "silly youngsters"
who'd usher in a new order. I suppose, vaguely, we believed that artists should inherit the universe.

One of my friends at the Academy took to composing
symphonies of odor, the foulest odors he could find and
produce, dedicating each work to the two governments.
Another created an artificial flower which would wilt if

touched; yet another gathered dung and baked it into likenesses of the Heads of State. My own contribution (halfhearted at best, I suppose) was the sculpting of single grains of sand, using the tools of my father, then scattering my invisible beauty in handfuls wherever I walked.

I'm not certain any longer what we really thought we were accomplishing. In our own words we were reacting, we were speaking out, we were being ourselves, we were caring. At any rate, this activity channeled our energies, made us work, made us think, let us live off of each other's various frenzies. It taught some of us, a few, that words and gestures get nothing done. Maybe somewhere, somehow, it accomplished something larger; I don't know. (I understand, by the way, that microsculpture is quite the thing in the academies today.) Such, anyway, was the temper and tempo of my youth.

When I was twenty, I left Ginh with my degrees and came to live in a small room up four flights of stairs here on Juhlz (my poem, *Crown of Juhlz*). I worked for a while as a tutor, then held a position at the old Empire Library, but came very soon to realize that I was unable to fit myself to a job of any sort.

I fled to Farthay, where I wrote my first novel and married. She was a young, small thing with joy in her heart and light in her eyes, a Vegan. Two years with me, and without the comfort of a child, was all she could bear. She left. It was best for both of us. We had already spent too much of our separate selves.

The rest of my life (I am 84) has been spent in forming and breaking idle patterns. I travel a lot, settle for short periods, move on (your letter retraced, and made me remember, many years of my life). What money I have comes through the kindness of friends; and from other, distant friends who buy my books.

My books: you ask after them. Thank you. Well, there's *Letters Home,* which I've already mentioned and which you've probably read. Quite against my own preferences and wishes, it has proved my most popular book; I've been told that it's taught in literature and sociology classes round about the Union.

There are the novels: *Day Breaks; Pergamum* (a sort of eulogy for my marriage); *A Throw of the Dice; Fugue and Imposition;* one or two others I'd just as soon not admit to.

Essays: *Pillow Saint; Halfway Houses; Arcadias; Avatars and Auguries.* Two volumes of letters between the Vegan poet Arndto and myself, concerning mostly Outworld poetry, entitled *Rosebushes* and *Illuminations.*

A collection of short stories, three volumes, *Instants of Desertion.*

And of course, the poems . . . *Overtures and Paradiddles; Misericords; Poems; Negatives; Abyssinia; Poems* again; *Printed Circuits; Assassins of Polish.* Some while back, I received a check with a letter informing me that a *Collected Poems* was to be issued through Union Press. I can't remember just how long ago that was, and can't know how long the message took to find me, so I don't know whether the book is available.

And coming at last to the poems you've sent, what am I to say? All critical intent is beyond me, I fear. I've been constantly bemused and confounded by what critics have found to praise and damn in my own work: I was aware neither that I had "narrowly ordered my sensibilities" nor that I "struck out boldly into the perilous waters that lie between a poetry of device and the poetry of apocalypse" (which another renders as aiming between "a poem of sentiment and one of structure"). Give me always the Common Reader, the sensitive ignorance.

("The perilous waters" . . . had I known there was danger of drowning, I might never have begun to write.)

You want Authority; I can give you none. Let me instead look up at these winter-blurred hills and say this: the poems you've sent, and which I return with this letter —they are not unique, but they speak of something which may come, something which may become yours alone.

Perhaps you have it now. But two years is a very short time.

They are direct, compact, all the flourishes are beneath the surface—things greatly to be praised in a young writer. In one line you are content to give shape, in another you pause and form; always something comes easy, to the ear, the eye, the tongue, the mind, the heart. Also to be admired.

You evidently achieve control with little struggle, effective structure with somewhat more difficulty (precision and accuracy are often separate things). But you have patience, and this will come. Your diction draws crisp, sharp lines around a poem, while imagery and resonance make what is contained soft and yielding. This is at least a proper direction. And I think you are right to work from the outside in, the way you seem to do.

Two years ago, when you wrote the letter, you were looking for an older, wiser, gentler voice than your own. I am sorry that I have been so long in admitting that I cannot provide it. Perhaps you've already found one, in some academy, some café. Or perhaps you no longer need it; edges have a way of wearing off. Peace, calm—but what I can give you is closer to a stillness.

I was quite moved by the Betelgeuse mood poems in particular: I should say that. I envy you these poems. Because of a late-developing nervous disorder, a clash in my mixed parentage, I am confined pretty much to Vega. I've not been outside the Combine since the day I came here. Something in the specific light complements my affliction, and I can go on in good health. But I believe I shall have to return to dark Earth before I die, that at least, in spite of all.

It occurs to me that you obviously know about writing, and I think you must have known the worth of your poems, so I can only assume that you are really asking about living. And I have one thing to say, a quiet thing: Ally yourself to causes and people, and you'll leave bits of yourself behind every step you take; keep it all, and you'll choke on it. The choice is every man's, for himself.

The day is wearing down, burning near its end. Lights have gone on, then off again, in the houses around me. Everyone is feeling alone.

So as darkness and winter move in, hand-in-hand, let me wish you the best of luck in your ambitions, apologize again for the delay, and bring to a close this letter, longer than any letter has a right to be.

And in closing, please accept again my thanks for your kind words. They are given so easily, yet mean so much, always.

Night now. Juhlzson birds have come off the lakes and out of forests, and are throbbing softly around me. The moons are sailing in and out of clouds. In a moment I shall move off the patio into the house. In a moment.

                                    Yours,
                              Samthar Smith

Here is an exuberant and funny story about death.

Here Is Thy Sting

by John Jakes

Sometimes, too, warmed by the fire, Shakespeare stayed downstairs all night . . .

"Rest, rest, don't fight so," Judith whispered to him once.

"I can't rest," he answered, "while the black beast waits for me."

—Robert Payne, *The Roaring Boys*

I

His brother came home from the Moon in an economy coffin, on a night when the meteorological bureau decided on rain. Something went wrong, as it frequently did. The April mist turned to a black, blinding downpour.

Through the shed's thick windows all peppered with rain, Cassius could just discern the vertical pillars of fire that grew thinner, thinner still, then flamed out. Rain hummed and slashed. It was a foul night for such a painful, intensely personal errand.

As the transport rocket settled into its concrete bed far out there, a dozen haul trucks raced from all directions toward its unfolding ramps. Then there seemed to be a collision. Headlamps tilted crazily. Men ran this way and that. A controller wigwagged his glowing red wands hysterically.

"Wild buncha cowboys," grumbled the Freight Customs official. "Next? Hey, you."

Parcels, crates, cylinders, drums were spilling down a dozen chutes from the rocket. Which was Timothy? Cassius turned from the window as the official called out again. He stepped up to the booth. The official's uniform was damp, wool-stinking. His expression was cross. Cassius recalled hearing the man ahead of him argue loudly with the official. He felt he should have chosen another queue, but it was too late.

"Okay, buddy, what's yours?"

"I'm picking up my brother," Cassius said.

The official mugged his disgust. "Oh for Christ's—the next shed is passenger, mister."

Cassius said, "You don't understand. My brother was —that is, he's dead. His body is on the rocket."

"Oh." The official blinked. "Name?"

"Cassius Andrews. Here's my News Guild card and my personal digit card if you need identification."

"His name, *his* name."

"The Reverend Timothy Andrews." Cassius tried to scan the upside-down manifest on the counter. "Maybe the shipment is listed under the Ecumenical Brothers. They paid his stipend at the Moon camp. He was stabbed trying to break up a knife fight between two miners, and the Brothers arranged to ship his—"

Reading down the lines, the official waved his hand to cut off the talk. Cassius felt sheepish. What did the man care about details of a family death? Nothing, of course.

When at last the official had ticked off the proper box with a checkmark and raised his dull eyes to stare through the wicket, he was no longer merely bored. He was plainly resentful. Of my mentioning dead people on such a miserable night? Cassius wondered.

"Mister," said the official, almost triumphantly, "whoever prepaid the body at Moonramp made a mistake. Underweighed by thirty-six pounds. There's extra duty due. Dozen point five credits."

Cassius fumbled inside his raincloak. "I'll be glad to pay it."

"You gotta see the adjustments manager. Three doors down. Next!"

The dismissal was so peremptory that Cassius, ordinarily a mild-tempered man, flushed. He was about to make a nasty retort. Then he recalled his own recurring dream. It tormented him twice or three times a week, regularly. He sighed and took the punched card from the official's hand.

Nobody liked to be bothered with death. Especially not in such rotten, depressing weather. Cassius could understand how the official felt.

Out another window he noticed that the haul truck tangle had been straightened out. The various crates, parcels and containers were being picked up by vehicles operated by the big and small land freight companies. Cassius had made no arrangements for transportation. But he'd been told that an on-the-spot haul service was for hire. He intended to send Timothy's body directly to the headquarters of the Brothers, where they had a chapel.

After the memorial service due all missionaries who died violent deaths—and many still did, in the lonely, rotgut-happy camps on the Moon and around Marsville Basin—Timothy would be interred with their mother and father in the family plot in Virginia. Timothy would have been, let's see, two years younger than Cassius, who was forty-two.

The adjustments manager had another client. Cassius lingered in the hall. He tried to restrain his impatience, then his anger. He had the eerie feeling that official stupidity was conspiring against him to delay the obligatory reunion with his brother.

After spending twenty minutes in the corridor, Cassius finally got to see the adjustments manager. The idiot didn't have the appropriate rate book at hand. That took another five minutes. Cassius paid the excess duty, watched while the manager thumbed his Hilton Bank card into a machine along with a triplicate invoice. At last he was given a pass to the pickup area.

He walked across the concrete in the slashing rain. He

had already decided that he'd damn well write an exposé of the mismanagement at Dulles Interplanetary and file it with the feature editor. God, there was enough bumbling bureaucracy here for ten exposés.

But the idea passed quickly.

Long ago Cassius had recognized and accepted his limitations. He seldom dreamed any more of writing *the* news story or series that would catapult him to fame.

There were eight hundred reporters on the *Capitol World Truth*. Out of these, a top dozen received around eighteen thousand credits per annum. They wrote all the exposé pieces of the type Cassius was imagining. Cassius himself earned a meager twelve two, almost the Guild minimum. Years ago he'd been slotted by Hughgenine, his editor, as a competent man to handle a section of the vast Alexandria suburban news beat. The Parent and Teaching Machine Association was his bailiwick. Well, he said to himself, the exposé was a good thought, anyway.

Dread came then.

The rain-soaked handler blinked at the receipt. "I seen it here a while ago, okay. But there ain't many items left and I don't see it now."

Cassius stared around the open shed. "I was delayed in the terminal. It must be here. It's a coffin."

"I know, I seen it. We had a real mess out here tonight, mister. Some jerky new driver rammed into a couple of the other pickup rigs. Maybe Elmo knows. Hey, Elmo?"

Elmo was fat and officious. "Sure, I seen it. The driver picked it up."

"What driver?" Cassius snapped.

"Just who the hell are you, mister?"

"The man's brother."

"Oh, okay. Keep your pants on." Elmo thumbed his flash. He riffled his tickets. Then he extended the packet, less blustery. "Ain't that the nuts? The part of the ticket showin' the name of the carrier is torn off. Oh boy, things are sure screwed up tonight, man, oh man."

Cassius raged and fumed and promised official vengeance for a full fifteen minutes. He turned out half the minor bureaucracy of the receiving department, to no good end. The coffin was gone.

Someone had stolen his brother's corpse.

"It's crazy!" he sputtered. Cowlike faces ringed him. "Who would steal a preacher's body? It's absolutely senseless."

No one answered. Cassius looked past the rain-lashed men. They were strangely nervous. Perhaps because of a theft; the rain; the accident and mix-ups and their obliviousness to the pickup driver. Or perhaps they were quiet because the situation had been further complicated by death.

Out beyond the concrete beds where the Sino-Russian Line was preparing to launch its evening shipment, Cassius saw the multileveled tangle of roads leading from the field, rising to merge with the ten broad lanes of the Washington Belt. Up one of those ramps and onto that highway had gone an unknown truck, carrying a stolen corpse.

"Crazy," Cassius said again. "You'll hear about this." He stalked off in the rain.

What indecent maniac would take such elaborate pains to pilfer the corpse of a man of God from a public place? Cassius was at once afraid he'd come in contact with some sinister group of madmen. Only later, when hindsight began to operate, did he analyze his reaction more deeply. He knew later that what had really troubled him was the fear that those who'd stolen the body were not crazy but perfectly, if esoterically, sane.

Lurching along in the rain, Cassius didn't know what he was going to do about the theft. But he was positive he was going to do something.

II

The trip to his apartment in Alexandria would require the better part of an hour. Cassius decided to put the time to use.

After he jockeyed his Ford Aircoupe to the hook-on with the magnetic strip, he dialed the tinted shell. The shell closed around the seat blister, shutting out the dazzle of thousands of headlamps in the oncoming lanes. Cassius rang up the headquarters of the Ecumenical Brothers in downtown Washington. The paper had paid for installing the minimum-screen visor in his car.

Presently a sleepy, clerical-collared face appeared.

"This is Reverend Tooker speaking. Yes?"

"I'm sorry to disturb you, Reverend."

"Quite all right. Tonight's my shift in the B-complex free kitchen. How can I help you?"

The cleric was unfamiliar. But so was Timothy's whole life, practically. Cassius hadn't seen his brother in twelve years. That didn't lessen his sense of duty and outrage:

"Reverend, I'm Cassius Andrews. I just came from Dulles where I planned to pick up Timothy's body. There seems to have been a mixup. Did you by any chance send a hauler from your building to fetch it?"

"No, Mr. Andrews. We understood you wished to take delivery. Wasn't our departed brother on the rocket?"

"He was. But somebody stole the coffin."

Reverend Tooker at once launched into theologically tinged commiseration. Cassius listened politely. But he knew he'd get no help from the white-haired divine. Most of Tooker's sincere and sympathetic talk about Timothy's service on the Moon, his dying a violent death in the service of the Creator and His Son, to Cassius was neither here nor there. Long ago he'd abandoned any concern with religion.

While the Reverend eulogized Timothy, Cassius drifted

off into other realms. Timothy had been a shy, dreamy boy in their childhood. He had been passionately religious, in contrast to Cassius who was passionately secular. For no special reason, Cassius was stung with somber recollections of his boyhood dreams of becoming a famous newsman and correspondent.

"—can only suggest you contact the police," Reverend Tooker concluded.

"Yes, I planned to do that next."

"Please come into the chapel at any time if we can be of help in your hour of trial," the Reverend said.

"Yes, I'll do that too, thanks." That was a lie. Cassius rang off. There was no point in telling the gentle, simple old fellow that he was becoming convinced Timothy's body had been pilfered by some sort of sex ghoul cult. A cult which—God help his brother—must be massively organized.

The Ford Aircoupe whizzed along on its thin pillars of air, halfway to Alexandria now. Cassius dialed the central police switchboard.

They were officially receptive, properly angry. Somehow, though, the conversation seemed routine. Cassius doubted the police would learn anything new when their operatives visited the freight sheds. The rain, the accident caused by the inexperienced driver, the resulting confusion, all had worked together to effectively blot out the trail of the body snatchers.

The Aircoupe was on the less crowded feeder belt over the polluted Potomac. The hour was growing late. In spite of that, Cassius dialed another number. He didn't want to be completely alone tonight. He found that Joy was home.

"That's terrible, Cassius," she said. He thought she was sincere. Joy was nearing forty, rather chubby-faced and a little ferret-eyed in the wrong light. Basically she was pretty, if grown stocky now that she'd given up hope of marriage and settled on a career. "Would you like me to come over?"

Rain hammered black, lonely, on the Aircoupe bubble.

"Could you, Joy? It'll take you an hour, I know. I really would like company. I can cook some eggs. You can stay the night."

"I wish I might, sweets. But the piece I'm working on is due tomorrow. I've unearthed some positively fantabulous little gimmicks in re what to do with leftover paper undies. They make the cutest buffers for a dusting robot and—oh dear. Forgive me. This is a terrible time to talk shop."

"That's all right." He forgave her. One of Joy's failings was a kind of compulsion to seek editorial paydirt in any situation, even lovemaking. Once in the middle of the night Joy had suddenly interrupted everything, sat up and jotted down some notes on a simply fantabulous position a housewife might use to relax her calf muscles. He added, "You don't have to stay the night, then."

"I can't, dear. As I say, this little piece is due. Cassius!"

"What, Joy?"

"You don't suppose there's anything in this theft, do you? Oh, I realize the moment is very trying for you. But could we make anything out of it?"

"I doubt that it's Joy de Veever's cup of tea," he replied. "Nor mine either. I also have a sinking feeling the cops are going to get nowhere. To tell the truth, Joy, this business has some nasty overtones. I'm not sure I want to pursue it myself."

The screened face grew bright-eyed. He might have been irritated if he hadn't understood that her query sprang from her compulsive professionalism. But only in part. He knew from their years of pleasant liaison that she was, at bottom, kindly.

"But you will pursue it, won't you, Cassius?"

"Yes, I suppose I must. Provided I can figure out where to turn next."

"We'll think of something. See you in an hour, sweets." And the screen blurred out.

Cassius occupied a one-room flat on the eighty-seventh floor of one of fifteen cluster buildings in a small Alexandria development. Decelerating for the hook-off, Cassius saw a familiar sprawl of towers just this side of his own project. The towers dwarfed the other units in the district. They were the local project of the Securo Corporation.

Securo, a private firm started ten years ago by a contractor and a professor of psychology, provided co-op living for young marrieds but added a fillip: all conceivable services, including mortgage, burial and educational insurance were included in one payment for the benefit of the occupants, who signed a lifetime contract. All across the country and everywhere abroad, Securo was building similar projects, but not fast enough for the demand.

Down at the paper, the boys, fancying themselves rather independent souls, referred to a Securo flat as a womb to tomb room, since many young parents were already willing their living space to their infants, to provide them maximum protection against the buffetings of fate.

Now, riding in the dark rain, Cassius shuddered a little as the lights of the Securo tract flashed past. There was something to be said for knowing you were protected, especially on unpleasant nights like this. And the newsmen weren't all that independent, either. The last Guild negotiations had lasted eighteen weeks, because management initially refused to include podiatry benefits in the package. Everyone wanted to be safe. Sometimes Cassius clucked his tongue, but sometimes too he sympathized.

Unlike Securo, Cassius's landlords offered only the standard auto, theft and major medical insurance with their flats. Cassius's place was a litter of books and the other paraphernalia of bachelor untidiness.

He opened two packages of Birdseye Brawny Breakfasts, watched while the fried eggs and bacon began to mushroom from the tiny white capsules. Joy wouldn't be arriving for a while yet. He drew the curtain around the cook unit and went to the bookcase to get his diary.

Faithfully he recorded the events of the evening. As a younger man he'd imagined he might be a latter-day Pepys. Now he wrote in the book out of habit more than anything, though occasionally he admitted to himself that what he was doing was hoping with words and phrases that a third-rate newspaperman could gain a slim remembrance after he died.

Someone might come across the diary among his effects, for instance. Recognize the burning perceptiveness and, lo! long after he was buried, elevate the name of Cassius Andrews to the heights of—

Rats. He knew it was idle foolishness. The prose was clear but mundane. It in no sense burned. Still, he wrote in the diary every night.

Joy de Veever arrived within an hour. Her evening wig, slightly awry, was an exotic purple to match her lip rouge. She hugged him briefly. They sat down to eat, Joy rather noisily and untidily. It was comforting to have her present.

Her real name was Joy Gollchuk. The editors believed, probably rightly, that Joy de Veever was the sort of by-line housewives preferred in a helpful hints column. She shared a cell at the *Capitol World Truth* with a pert sixty-year-old grandmother named Mrs. Swartzmore, who reviewed films under the name Ma Cine.

"Really (munch munch), Cassius (swallow), this is the most despicable type thing I've ever (swallow) heard of. Stealing a body indeed! A Holy Joe's body, too."

"I don't get mad about the minister part so much as over the fact that he was my brother. I feel an obligation not to let the whole thing pass."

"Maybe (swallow) it's some sort of obscene ring operating."

"I've wondered that. It's actually the reason I'm slightly leery of pushing too far. But I know in the long run I can't let the possibility stop me."

"Tell me again what the police said."

"That they'll do their best. I don't doubt it. But I was

there tonight, Joy. The handlers felt sorry about it, sure. Things were obviously in such a confused state that they could do nothing beyond what they did. Which was, admit someone drove in, picked up Timothy's coffin with false papers, then drove away again."

Joy's eyes glittered. She leaned near. "Did you ask for police cooperation?"

"Didn't I just tell you?"

"Not about that, silly. I mean cooperation in case there's a juicy story behind—oh. You're offended."

"No I'm not."

"Juicy was a bad word. I'm sorry, sweets. But there might be a piece in it for you, Cassius. Sort of a memorial to your brother, you might say," hastily justifying herself. "After all, dear, let's face it. You're not the world's hottest reporter. You could use some self-promotion."

"Joy, after a while a man knows what he is and isn't."

"Oh come on, Cassius! Don't you have any drive to assert yourself?"

He thought of the diary. He glanced at a collection of file card holders on the self-suspending bookshelves. He frowned.

"Of course. But it doesn't come out in trying to make hay from what's happened to Timothy."

Joy crunched a last morsel of bacon. "Well, you certainly won't do yourself any good with that silly biography you've been working on for six years. The poor man's been written about in eleven different volumes."

"Twelve," Cassius corrected. "As you know, I've discovered some new angles which might—"

"Enshrine you with posterity?" Joy smiled. "Cassius, really."

"I wasn't going to say that."

"It's what you meant, though."

"Joy, I like working on the book," he said. "How did we get on this subject?"

For a moment anger sparked in his rather downturning

brown eyes. He controlled the anger. Not a major effort at all. He gripped her hand across the fold-up table.

"Joy, if I didn't know so well that you can't help hunting for angles any more than a cat can help chasing a mouse, I'd get damned mad at you sometimes."

"Yes, you do understand me," she said gently. "Which is more than I do for you most of the time, I must confess."

He squeezed her hand. "Thanks for coming tonight."

"I apologize for calling your book silly, dear."

"I don't mind. So long as you realize I'll keep right on working on it."

For a moment Joy's eyes were shadowed. "Still have the dream?"

"Yes."

"That's the reason for the book, isn't it?"

"Um, partly, I guess."

"I don't have any dreams like that, Cassius. But I suppose I run after stories for the same reason too."

"Yes."

Suddenly she snapped her fingers. The cocktail zircon on her right hand flashed back the rays of the solar panels which lit the room. "I just had the most marvelous idea. If you get no satisfaction from the police, why don't you go right to the W.B.I?"

"Are you out of your mind? I don't know anybody down there."

"What difference does that make? Go straight to the director himself! If you ask me, Cassius, this theft sounds downright sinister. Maybe the Neo-Leninists are making a comeback."

"And you suggest I waltz right in and state my case to Flange himself?"

"That's not as impossible as it sounds. I was talking to Charlie Pelz yesterday over morning vitamins."

"Charlie Pelz?"

"Oh, you know. He does those Black Museum pieces on Sundays for the true-crime nuts. Charlie said he was down to the W.B.I. Building last week and it's practically turned into an old people's home. Offices empty. Men sitting around doing nothing. He asked whether he could see Flange's assistant a moment, to get a comment on a story he was writing, and he almost dropped over when the secretary said Flange had no appointments all day, why didn't Charlie talk to him? So you try him. Maybe this unstable world peace is more stable than we think."

Cassius chewed his lip. "I don't know who could set it up for me."

"I tell you, Charlie Pelz said no one had to set it up! Flange was so *un*busy even a bootboy could get in to see him."

Although he rejected the idea as slightly ludicrous, Cassius nevertheless filed it away. He and Joy finished their caffeine water with a rehash of the mysterious events out at Dulles. It got them nowhere. She kissed him neatly and rather moistly on the cheek, squeezed his arm, and he ushered her to the door.

"Must run, sweets, but I do hope you sleep well. Try not to fret over what's happened."

"I have to find out what happened to Timothy, Joy. I must."

"Of course. Take my suggestion, though. Thinking about the W.B.I. And Cassius—" Again the eyes, rimmed in purple mascara, glittered. Consolation went out the window, replaced by professionalism. "—if there is anything in it, a hot tidbit either one of us could use—oh, I know I sound terribly crass, but after all, you have only one life to live and you have to make the best of it."

"That's right," Cassius said, hiding laughter. "Good night, Joy. And thanks."

Poor girl, he thought when she'd gone. Imagines one day *the* story will fall into her lap. He'd never had the courage to tell her, as she repeatedly told him, that her talent was small.

Oh, she could do a major story, all right. But the material for the story would have to drop from heaven. She'd never find it picking around among new uses for paper undies in the home. Perhaps he'd continued their liaison so long because, unlike Joy, he had realized his personal limits and therefore could feel gently, privately superior.

After a vigorous rubdown with a pre-wetted shower cloth he pulled a switch. His bed rose from the floor. He awoke an hour later, snuffling and breathing violently, an ache in his chest.

The dream had returned.

III

It was a dream of himself running, mile after slow-motion mile, while the dog snapped at his heels.

The dog was twice as long as a man. Its claws were like sharp iron files. Its fangs were like white spikes. Its yellow eyes were the only two blazes of color in the gray waste where he was pursued.

He'd dreamed the dream regularly for about six years. It had begun about the time he had first noticed at cocktail parties that people were talking with low voices and embarrassed laughter about how short all the days seemed, how rapidly they flew. People his own age. He knew what the dog represented.

Knowing, however, didn't relieve the after-effects of the nightmare. It only intensified them.

Hastily Cassius threw back the coverlet. He turned on the lights and started to work cross-indexing notes and snippets for his book. The project was probably futile, as Joy maintained. Twelve books had been published on the same subject already.

The book was to be a biography of Colonel Robin Delyev. He was the officer responsible for leading the combined American-Russian shock forces which repelled the initial invasion of Puerto Rico by the Chinese, sixty years ago. All Delyev and his thousand troops had to work with was a storehouse full of antiquated U.S. personal missile launchers.

Poring and poking at the National Archives, Cassius had stumbled across some new materials. They had been misfiled: seven hitherto unpublished letters, four long, three no more than notes but revealing nonetheless, written by Delyev to the Pentagon just before the Colonel's death. Headily Cassius had realized that none of the other twelve biographers had included the letters. And they added fresh insights into Delyev's brilliant deployment of his meager forces.

The majority of the book Cassius planned to draw from the secondary sources, re-slanting it to his own rather scholarly, restrained style of writing. The volume would contain most of the anecdotes already available, such as the one about the night in the Chinese consulate in Chicago, before the war, when Delyev drank too much and made the epigrammatic speech which earned him the nickname "Old Rattling Rockets." But the book, his book alone, would also contain the seven letters. Provided he finished the draft fairly soon, and got it submitted to a publisher.

Cassius knew that even when the volume was published, if it ever was, it would be relatively obscure in the crowded market; read only by those faithful who would always buy one more work on a subject that interested them. Cassius had no illusions. But he did believe that the fresh insights contained in the letters might add one small grain of truth to the world's accumulation as it related to the dead Delyev.

Besides, the book almost demanded to be written, worthy or not. It demanded writing especially in the lonely hours after he dreamed about the slavering dog who ran so slowly, yet so remorselessly, at his heels.

He labored on, a lonely figure in his small box of an apartment, alone in the night, alone in the rain, ignored but uncaring, until he finally crawled back to bed around four and slept untroubled until dawn.

Next day, he conferred personally with the Washington police.

They were investigating, yes, certainly. But to be honest, they'd interviewed several dozen people at Dulles and gotten nowhere. They would certainly keep trying, yes. There might be something decidedly sinister behind the theft. They would call him.

At lunch in the newspaper mess, Joy reminded him about the W.B.I. Cassius felt a little silly. But the obvious impending failure of the local police angered him. He took the afternoon off and rode the belts over.

As Charlie Pelz had promised, he was admitted to the Director's office without question or hesitancy. And to fulfill the rest of the prophecy, Cassius actually felt exactly like falling over on his face in utter surprise.

Not over getting in. Over what he saw after he got there.

IV

R. Ripley Flange, the mastiff-chinned Director of the World Bureau of Investigation, was sitting at his broad desk, feet up, throwing darts.

One whizzed perilously close to Cassius's head as he closed the door. Cassius flinched. The iron spike of the dart thudded into the door. On it a paper bull's-eye had been nailed, the large nails carelessly driven into the lustrous patina of the obviously antique and priceless wood. Even the newly-refurbished White House had been pannelled in polystyrene. For a genuine wood door to be pocked with thousands of dart and nail holes amounted to desecration.

"Sorry," Flange said. He grinned in a sleepy way. "I'm rather on the track of a big one. Fourteen bull's-eyes this morning. Best yet."

Edgily, Cassius sat down. The Director sighed, laid aside his dart case and tented his hands. He tried to frown with interest. Cassius had the uncanny feeling that the Director was peering straight through him, as though he were one of those model-kit men, wholly transparent.

"What can I do for you, sir? Care to apply for a position as a special operative? We have dozens of openings." The heavy lips, which had once sneered so heroically out of simulcast screens during the lectures on Chinese subversion in the bedding industry, now pursed out in what Cassius could only describe as a careless, thoroughly lazy way.

"No, sir, I didn't come about a job."

"Some crime then, I'll bet." Flange sounded unhappy. "Isn't that it?"

"I hate to bother you, sir. The local police seem so overburdened, and unable to make any headway. You see, sir, my brother's body has disappeared."

"Pity." Flange was restlessly eyeing a wall bookcase in which stood nearly a hundred copies of the inexpensive five-credit polybound edition of Flange's magnum opus, *Alert! The Yellow Underground Is Attacking.* "I'm certain we can help you. Many more resources open these days. Laboratories, so forth. International crime, I take it?"

"I'm not sure what it is, sir. Perhaps I should talk to someone else in the Bureau."

"No, no, I'll handle it." Flange frowned. "I suppose it is my responsibility, after all. Now where are those damned forms?"

And he grumbled and rumbled through his desk, his hands shaking in a palsied way. Cassius fidgeted. He felt hot, embarrassed. There was something wrong with the old fellow. Where was the lion's roar for justice, the eagle's scream for watchfulness? Gone was the ferocity that had made Flange a legend, whether you cared for his style of operation or not.

At last the Director produced a paper, incredibly frayed.

"Well, I found one report form, anyway. I'd send you

to someone else, except my deputy director has gone to
Las Vegas and I haven't heard from him in four months.
That's all right, though. He needed a rest."

Cassius had an urge to bolt and run. Had the W.B.I.
turned into a rest home for its obviously mentally infirm
chief?

"Something about a brother's body, wasn't it?" said
Flange.

The peculiar situation would have been laughable had
Cassius not suspected there was something unpleasant
lurking just under the surface. Flange's weird mood made
it impossible for him to generate very much righteous
rage as he rattled off a bare sketch of the mixup at Dulles
Interplanetary, the theft of Timothy's remains. Once in a
while Flange's pen jerked, marking appropriate box or
space.

"Distressing," Flange said at the end, with patent insin-
cerity. "Yes, I see. Body theft."

"I thought it might possibly have some international
implications. That's why I came to you. Of course I'm
also anxious personally to make whoever did it pay up."

"Naturally. We'll put our best men on it right away.
What's your office digit?"

Cassius repeated the eighteen numerals which included
his extension. While Flange wrote down the figures with
his right hand, his left strayed like a spider over to the
dart case, then drummed on the edge. Cassius rose
abruptly. He couldn't stand any more. The old man was
senile and no one had the heart to remove him from office, that was it.

Also, Cassius felt with a certainty that stoked his determination to a new height, that R. Ripley Flange had no
intention of putting his best men on it. Or maybe even
any men, period. The Washington police wanted to try
but were overworked. Flange simply didn't care.

"Visor you as soon as we have anything. Get right on
it, yes we will." Flange was slumped in his throne chair

like a punctured balloon. His hand drummed on the dart case, drummed.

"Don't you want any more details? I only gave you the essentials a minute ago." Flange, though obviously sick, was beginning to infuriate him.

"We have enough, we have plenty, best men. Visor you."

After several weeks Cassius even gave up hoping. He discussed it over vitamins with Charlie Pelz one afternoon. Charlie agreed that things were sure strange at the W.B.I. The place appeared understaffed. Moribund. He could offer no explanation other than the one Cassius had already come up with—Flange was such a fixture that the government was almost conscience-bound to await his death with something like unquestioning reverence.

Cassius agreed. He thought privately that it was distressing to watch the disintegration of a person's drive as old age crept in.

But Cassius didn't badger Flange or the W.B.I. Indeed, he forgot them. At the end of the fourth week following Timothy's disappearance, a few other curious things had pushed their way into his mind. They had no bearing on Timothy, probably. But they were the kinds of things which he, on the paper, was in a position to pursue a bit without the aid of sad old men who were once mighty tigers but who were now all gums and no guts.

What first put Cassius on the trail was the peculiar and shocking concert of Madame Kagle.

V

By intermission the shock was profound. Cassius noted its beginnings in the unusual amount of head-turning while Madame Kagle ran through *The Joint M.I.T. Faculty Sonata*, never missing a note but missing the fire of it altogether.

No one was so impolite as to gasp during the second selection, Oodner's *Peripheral Stimuli*. But Cassius saw mouths hanging open all up and down his row. No music critic, Cassius had nevertheless seen plenty of photos of the celebrated Kagle attack. At its best it was a savagely bow-shaped posture above the keyboard of the harpsivac. It emphasized the woman's boniness and made her resemble, some said, a fairy-tale witch maniacally searching for the touchstone in a casketful of junk beads. Out of such agonized personal involvement, great music was wrenched.

Except this evening.

Madame Wanda Kagle sat perfectly straight. She was watching the one hundred thirty-six keys, all right. But she was glass-eyed. Her mouth, like many in the audience, hung open in a peculiar slack-lipped indifference. The applause at the end of the first half of the program was thin.

Stumbling and shoving up the aisle for a quick smoke, Cassius and Joy heard all around them whispered comments such as: "Unbelievable." "Lackluster." "Crushingly disappointing." They pushed out into the vast foyer of the Sports Dome. The roof was rolled back to the stars and warm night breezes. Joy waited for her smoke to pop fire, inhaled and said:

"The old babe must be close on sixty. Wonder if she's slipping. Maybe she has to key up with amphets, and forgot."

"That's a bad pun," Cassius said. "I'd guess she was loaded with booze if it wasn't common knowledge that she very nearly lives like a saint. I read somewhere that she's even tried hypnotism to push everything out of her mind but her music."

"She certainly succeeded," Joy answered. "That was pure claptrap in there. She couldn't have been less interested."

"This puts a little different complexion on going to the reception afterward," Cassius mused. "Ordinarily I

wouldn't be much interested in using those chits Greeheim gave you along with the tickets. I don't know beans
about music. Or about how to get along with musical co-
teries, either."

Joy's eyes glittered. "For God's sake, Cassius, you can
pretend, can't you? You could even make 'em think
you're the regular critic. Fake it a little. Just sneer.
Greeheim isn't that well known yet. He's only been with
the paper a few months. I certainly don't want to insult
him when he gets over his illness by telling him we used
the tickets but not the party passes."

The crowd was beginning to stir, pushing back to the
entrance ramps for the second half. "You won't have to
tell him," Cassius grinned. "In the light of that first half, I
wouldn't miss seeing Madame K. close up for anything.
Maybe we'll get a hint of what's wrong with her."

"Now you're talking!" Joy said, eyes sharp as awls.

As they fought the aisle battle on the way to their
seats, Cassius considered telling Joy the real reason for
his curiosity. She was on one of her imaginary scents
again, hoping she'd unearth some hot exclusive. While
Cassius, on the other hand, had stared at Madame Kagle
and seen something else entirely—

A ghostly twin image of the vast, weary indifference of
R. Ripley Flange.

Lights dimmed. Madame Kagle appeared from the
wings. She seemed to stumble. Like a sleepwalker she approached the bench of the harpsivac. She sat down. She
dry-washed her hands, as if warming them. Joy was noisily rippling the pages of the program, twisting it to get
light. She hissed, "Oh boy, this'll be fantabulous. *The Algebraic Suite*. It's one of my favorites."

But there was to be no *Algebraic Suite*. Madame Kagle
seemed frozen at the console. A look of supreme sorrow
came onto her aging features. It was immediately replaced by a sly, mocking smile. Moving with the painful
lethargy of the arthritic—which she definitely was not—
Madame Kagle rose. She circled the harpsivac and

yanked the plug from the floor socket. The thousands of tiny multicolored lights on the banked tonal computers simultaneously went black.

Madame Kagle cast a tired glance at the shocked audience. She lifted her right shoulder in the smallest shrug. She sauntered off the stage.

Once the curtain dropped and the impossible became a fact, the crowd was as silent as mourners entering a mortuary. There were hushed little speculations about narcotics, insanity, sex, religion, gall bladder, dropsy, thrombosis, poor investment counseling and so forth. People seemed reluctant to move from the foyer onto the broad piazza outside the Sports Dome. Only a few drifted from the piazza toward the parking docks.

"Wow," Joy whispered, "I can't wait to get the dirt at the reception."

Cassius was about to speak when the annunciator horn of a newsvend machine rolling through the crowd blared that everyone mustn't forget that next Monday was D-Day, and that details on the free city-wide immunizations against scaling scalp could be had by inserting a coin in the slot. The contraption dinned the fact that its papers contained a full list of the twenty-two hundred dispensaries which would be set up to distribute the free capsules to inoculate the populace against the dread scourge. The drive was the latest work of the ancient March of Quarters Foundation. Details, details inside—

Blaring, the machine trundled on. Rubbing his ear, Cassius answered Joy by saying, "Suppose we don't find out. Suppose Madame Kagle doesn't show up. Perhaps she's ill."

"Somebody'll be there who knows the score. Come on, Cassius, get the car."

As they wormed through the stunned throng on the piazza, voices rippled suddenly in excitement. Cassius and Joy craned around. Down the performer's ramp a sleek, expensive Rolls-Fujica air limousine was gliding, fast. People were crossing the ramp now. The chauffeur was forced to apply the brakes. That was when the yellow-cheeked bootboy, probably the son of some Chinese war refugee, fell off the piazza balustrade.

The lad had been up there brushes in hand, chanting in a singsong about shining the dress boots of gentlemen. Somehow he slipped, just as the Rolls-Fujica came to a halt.

"He's dead," a woman cried. The crowd, herd-like, shifted. Joy couldn't resist. Cassius was dragged along.

For a moment the scene was very vivid to him. The drop from the balustrade to the main ramp was twenty feet or more. By some twist of fate the bootboy had hit skull first on the prestressed poly. He lay with his red and gray brains smashed out. Meantime the Rolls-Fujica had started up.

The performer's ramp crossed the main one, on which the bootboy lay, at the piazza corner. A blur of motion in the aircar tonneau caught Cassius's eye. He saw Madame Kagle order her chauffeur to stop again. Her face strained to the window. Of all the curious who were gasping and oh-ing over the accident, she alone seemed truly moved.

The Rolls-Fujica sped on. Cassius shuddered. The woman's eyes had mirrored some pure hell even he couldn't see.

"Wonder if there's a human interest bit in it," Joy said.

"Joy, for God's sake don't be so callous."

She smiled. "It is one of my failings, isn't it, sweets? All right, first things first. But let's hurry. We don't want to miss the reception."

The reception, they discovered, was already going full blast in one of the larger private function halls of The Hotel of the Three Presidents. Passing under an arch decorated with a bust of one member of the trio—they were entering the Edward Room—Joy grabbed his arm.

"Cassius, look! The old girl's here. And drunker than a hoot owl, it seems."

"I don't like this a damn bit," he muttered.

"Oh, for heaven's sake, why not?"

"It just seems like a wake before you have a dead body."

"Don't be so squeamish. I wouldn't miss it for anything."

Joy pulled and tugged until they were past the coat robot, through the champagne line and lurking at the fringe of a small crowd surrounding Madame Kagle. The lady virtuoso was indeed pretty well gone. She staggered around like a scarecrow off its pole. Nobody was laughing, though. Not the socialites, not the critics. The mood was one of acute embarrassment.

Madame Kagle seemed to be centering most of her remarks on a ruddy-faced priest of middle years. Joy whispered that the priest was a well-known expert on sacred music. Madame Kagle was waving her champagne glass back and forth under the priest's long-suffering nose. Each wave threatened to douse him.

"—and I say you still haven't answered my question, Father Bleu."

"Haven't I, dear lady? I thought I stated that death is merely the beginning of—"

"No, no, *no!*" Her voice was high as a harpy's. "Don't go all gooey and metaphysical. I mean to ask, what is death the act, the situation, the moment?"

She watched him foxily. The priest in turn struggled to remain polite. "Madame, I'm not positive I follow."

"Let me say it another way. Most people are afraid of dying, yes?"

"I disagree. Not those who find mystical union with the body of Christ in—"

"Oh, come off it!" Madame Kagle shrilled. "People are frightened of it, Father Bleu. Frightened and screaming their fear silently every hour of every day they live. Now I put it to you. Of what are they afraid? Are they afraid of the end of consciousness? The ultimate blackout, so to speak? Or are they afraid of another aspect of death? The one which they can't begin to foresee or understand?"

"What aspect is that, Madame Kagle?"

"The pain." She glared. "The pain, Father. Possibly sudden. Possibly horrible. Waiting, always waiting somewhere ahead, at an unguessable junction of time and place. Like that bootboy tonight. How it must have hurt. One blinding instant when his head hit, eh? I suggest, Father Bleu, *that* is what we're afraid of, *that* is the wholly unknowable part of dying—the screaming, hurting how, of which the when is only a lesser part. The how is the part we never know. Unless we experience it."

She slurped champagne in the silence. She eyed him defiantly.

"Well, Father? What have you got to say?"

Discreetly Father Bleu coughed into his closed fist. "Theologically, Madame, I find the attempt to separate the mystical act of dying into neat little compartments rather a matter of hairsplitting. And furthermore—"

"If that's how you feel," she interrupted, "you're just not thinking it out."

"My good woman!" said Father Bleu gently.

"Pay attention to me!" Madame Wanda Kagle glared furiously. "I say you pay attention! Because you have never stopped to think about it, have you? If death resembles going to sleep, why, that's an idea your mind can get hold of. Isn't it? You may be afraid of it, yes. Afraid of the end of everything. But at least you can get hold of some notion of something of what it's like. Sleep. But can you get hold of anything of what it must feel like to experience the most agonizing of deaths? Your head popping open like that bootboy's tonight, say? A thousand worms of pain inside every part of you for a second long as eternity? Can you grasp *that*? No, you can't, Father Bleu. And that's what death is at its worst—the unknown, the possibly harrowing pain ahead."

She clamped her lips together smugly. She held out her champagne glass for a refill. A woman in furs clapped a hand over her fashionably green lips and rushed from the group. Though puzzled, Joy was still all eyes and ears.

"Even your blessed St. Paul bears me out, Father."

The priest glanced up, startled. "What?"

"The first letter to the Corinthians, if I remember. The grave has a victory, all right. But it's death that has the sting."

In the pause the furnace doors behind her eyes opened wide, and hell shone out.

"I know what I'm talking about, Father. I've been there."

Slowly she closed her fingers, crushing the champagne glass in her hand. Weeping, blood drooling from her palm down her frail veined arms, she had to be carried out.

The party broke up at once.

The gloom was even deeper than at the Dome. "Wait'll Greeheim gets a load of this dirty linen!" Joy whispered as they left.

Later, when Cassius escorted Joy to the door of her flat, she held out her cheek for a routine buss. But her mind was elsewhere. "I certainly wonder what Greeheim will make of that nutty harangue. Artistic temperament?"

"It's an interesting notion, anyway."

"What is?"

"Oh, there being two elements in death. The sleep and the pain. I wonder which one you really do fear most. I never thought about it before."

She patted his cheek. "And because you never think about really sensational story material like funeral rackets or sewage control graft, Cassius my love, you'll never get anywhere in our particular little rat-race. But that's all right. I like you just the same. Good night. Thanks for a fantabulous evening."

Waiting for the tube to take him down, Cassius was struck again by an eerie feeling. It wasn't so much the peculiarity of Madame Kagle's statements. They were pretty obtuse, after all. It was the queer resemblance he saw, or thought he saw, between her attitude and that of R. Ripley Flange. Somehow his mind wanted to equate the jerked plug with the dart case. It was almost as though the pair of them had had exactly the same lunatic vision, whatever it might be.

But the matter really had no relation to the problem still nagging him, he realized. The problem of Timothy's disappearance.

I've been there. The woman's words stayed in his mind the rest of the evening. What could they possibly mean?

Dutifully he recorded the unusual affair in his diary, then put in some time on the notes for his book. The dream of the dog at his heels was even more intense than usual. He awoke near dawn, wringing with sweat. Three cups of caffeine water were required before he was fully awake and free of the grip of the nightmare.

As he went to work he remembered once having read something about Madame Kagle's brother. Later in the day he had to go to the paper's morgue on another story. He looked up the Kagle name just out of curiosity. In addition to much material on Madame Wanda, there were several clips on her younger brother. The last of them stated that Dr. Frederic Kagle, a renowned neurosurgeon, had resigned from the World Institutes of Health to enter private practice. The clip was three years old.

Maybe, Cassius laughed to himself, the poor old woman had been put through the wringer by her brother in the cause of science. He laughed again, envisioning the usual horrific collection of apparatus, electrodes and blue lightnings that leapt from point to point while the demon doctor looked on and tittered.

The wool-gathering did have one solid result, surprisingly. It got Cassius to speculating again about a new angle on Timothy's fate.

Originally Cassius had wondered whether the body had been purloined by some unspeakable sex ring. Now he had another notion, no doubt equally off base but at least remotely possible. There was no connection with Dr. Frederic Kagle. It was only that Kagle's obscurity suggested scientists who, for one reason or another, were forced to work in absolute anonymity.

A third time Cassius laughed at himself in the gray loneliness of the morgue's reading cubicle. The medical body-snatcher bit in this day and age? Ridiculous.

Or was it?

Was the government, for instance, preparing some new superweapon in fear of possible disintegration of the tenuous Sino-Caucasian Peace? Something compelled him to take down the morgue index book. He leafed through until he located the proper heading. *Disappearances, Unsolved.*

He used the keyboard to code the paper tape. The tape vanished down a slot. A humming. Cassius was startled when not one but three microfilm spools popped from the tube.

There was always a routine number of unexplained disappearances within any given period. Distraught offspring. Erring husbands. Crimes that never saw the light of day. So he expected one spool at the most. He fed the first spool into the view box.

He did find that customary expected number of accounts of vanishing humanity. He also found thirteen instances of the disappearance of dead bodies within the last twenty-four months.

His brother Timothy was the last of the thirteen. He was represented by his obit and a two-paragraph item in the *Capitol World Truth*. The item covered the jetport incident. Cassius had seen it several times.

He double-checked each spool again. He hadn't misread. The thirteen who were gone had died in a uniform way.

By violence.

VI

Almost one year to the day after the theft of Timothy Andrews' body, the sovereign and somewhat backward state of New York prepared to let Butcher Balk have five hundred thousand volts. Cassius was waiting.

He was waiting in the prison burial ground on the Hudson bluffs, hunched down in his Ford Aircoupe. The vehicle was parked in a growth of budding maples to one side of a small service road. The time was 10:05 P.M.

Theoretically, Butcher Balk had been dead five minutes. April snow swirled, a quaint effect, courtesy of the weather bureau. Cassius was glad for the white scatter. It would afford him extra concealment in the dark, he hoped.

In order to be here this evening Cassius had been forced to lie both to Joy and his editor Hughgenine. He complained of a spell of male post-equinoctial depression, a common burden of urban life any more. Three other times in the year that had just passed he had also gone off following his elusive suspicions. On those occasions he had pleaded acute hangover, g.i. distress and bucket-seat hip, respectively.

Each time he'd figured that at last he was right. Each time he had been wrong. Worse, there was nothing to suggest tonight would be different.

But he refused to give up.

The first time, he'd traveled all night to reach Watkins Glen. The Continental driving star Baron von Pfalz had smashed up his Sonic Special in the Grand Prix, dying in a multi-car wreck on the chicane. Cassius had felt like a ghoul loitering around the little chapel where the other racers and mechanics held a memorial for the Baron. A sobbing woman, three children in tow, took von Pfalz's corpse away in a hearse. Cassius drove home keenly disappointed.

The following week the sports section of the *Capitol World Truth* carried a photo of the little family beside the Baron's grave plot. The woman and children, then, had not been actors.

So it went twice more: complete failure in outguessing them. Whoever *they* were.

The second occasion, no one tried to snatch the corpse of Dolly Sue Wei, the first non-American ever to register at the University of Levittown. She entered her first class flanked by the drawn pistols of U.N. marshals. Cassius had been sure the situation would produce violence. It did. Next night someone threw a sharp rock and Dolly died of brain damage.

But she was buried in a routine way in a free cemetery in Manhattan's Oriental ghetto. Cassius was there.

He had also rushed to a mortuary in New Jersey just last February. The Great Rococo, a stage magician, had died with the back of his head shot off while performing the bullet catch before a convention of Moose. Buried without incident in Tenafly.

The three blind alleys might have led another man to abandon the search. But Cassius had access to the paper's morgue. There he convinced himself he wasn't a lunatic.

In the interval during which he'd guessed wrong and gone on fruitless chases, the bodies of five other men—a film star, a slum pastor, an insurance salesman pushing his car to two hundred on the Interstate, a hunter after possum in Kentucky, a suicide in Cleveland—had all disappeared before interment.

Now, in the snowy night, Cassius brooded over his lack of success in outguessing *them*. Yet he was certain *they* were still in operation, and it was merely a matter of time before—

Thinking, he failed to see the drop of the translucent gray force wall of Ossining's new Bartlow Martin wing. He saw the headlights, though. They threw yellow up the hillside. The burial gang was on its way.

The outer wall shimmered up into place again, hiding a ghostly flag on the nine-hole therapy course. Speedy and efficient, the corpse handlers parked the truck on the other side of a low knoll. They rolled the gravedigger from the truck. They lowered the plain poly coffin containing the remains of Butcher Balk into the pre-dug hole. They turned on the digger and stood back while it went to work pitching on earth, its eight metal arms wigwagging black across a spotlight on the truck's cowl.

Unobserved, Cassius spied from his Aircoupe. He'd selected Butcher Balk as a likely target because the killer had received so much publicity. Of course, that might frighten *them* away. But the publicity said Butcher Balk had no living relatives. And that was another part of the pattern Cassius thought he'd discovered.

In six instances the disappearing dead people had also been survivorless. In other cases Cassius couldn't tell; no mention was made in the printed obits, but since they were wire service items, that didn't necessarily rule out the possibility of no relatives.

Snow swirled. The gravedigger flashed its green light and retracted its arms. Butcher Balk was a safecracker who had been rehabilitated after his first manslaughter conviction. His adjusted personality had been imperfect, had cracked, had resulted in a berserk massacre of ten men, women and children one Sunday afternoon in a hamlet on the St. Lawrence. Hence the seldom-given maximum penalty. Now Butcher Balk was only a faint mound among other mounds under the fresh snow.

The prison wall field sank. The truck vanished. The wall went up. Silence and the snow claimed the ghostly Hudson cliffs.

"If Joy could see me," Cassius said aloud, to keep himself company, "she'd think I was completely gone."

The hours passed. Eleven o'clock. Twelve. One. One-thirty. Cassius was convinced he'd made another wrong guess. He was ready to abandon the whole project. He took out the laminated card embossed with his personal digit, poised it over the ignition slot.

Two red-dusky eyes opened below.

He knuckled the weariness out of his eyesockets, looking again. The eyes were headlamps, large ones. But with reddish lenses for snow- and rain-probing radar.

Instantly Cassius began to sweat and gnaw his lip. The murky red circles would be invisible from the prison. He had difficulty seeing them himself. Radar lamps indicated a very costly vehicle. Something with a lot of equipment inside, like the mobile surgery and consultation rooms so many personal-injury lawyers drove. Gently Cassius levered up the vent in the Aircoupe blister.

He thought he heard voices. He certainly heard the gutter and clank of a machine. They'd brought their own gravedigger.

Twice its black arms flashed across the circles of the red radar lenses, illusory, quick as a blink. Cassius was now desperately afraid the thieves were vicious mobsters, revanchist foreign agents or something equally deadly. He slipped the card into the slot, heard the compressors begin to whoosh. Gently, gently, he levered the Aircoupe out of parking contact with the ground, ready to race in pursuit.

The thieves took twice as long as the prison detail. From this Cassius inferred they had dug up the coffin, then replaced the earth so their work would go undetected. As the thoroughness of their operation hit him, he found himself suddenly pumped full of adrenalin and rage. When the radar lenses vanished, indicating the truck's departure, he was ready.

He jerked the Aircoupe into forward. He picked them up on the feeder leaving the burial ground.

Apparently because of the snow or the solitude of the countryside or both, they never suspected he was roughly a mile behind them on the long trip over the state line into Westport, one of the cancerous slums affixed to the body of Greater Manhattan.

The truck whizzing along on its air jets finally slowed on a seamy street. It pulled into the side drive of a ramshackle funeral parlor and disappeared in the rear. Under a lonely mercury light a sign reading COMMUTER'S REST MORTUARY CHAPEL stood on the unkempt, snow-patched lawn.

Cassius cruised half a block down, parked and waited. The truck never came out.

The windows of the place were black. Painted over? There was absolutely no sign of life. As false dawn broke, Cassius got away from there. He relaxed only when he was on the Washington Belt North. He licked his lips, fought his tiredness, struggled with what he must do next.

The police?

Yes, that was the sensible answer. But something in him rebelled.

After all, he'd invested nearly a year on the chase, which was now hotting up considerably. Had Timothy not been involved, he'd have reported to the authorities at once. But the authorities hadn't done much of anything for him the first time. He still resented it.

Had he the guts to carry it one step more and see what happened?

Well, maybe he hadn't the guts. But he had the will. Months of frustration had developed it.

Once back in his flat, he was bothered again. He was the only person who knew the location from which the ring operated. Whom could he tell? Joy?

He warned himself off. Fond as he was of Joy, he knew his lady-love would try to convert the dross of a personal cause into the gold of self-promotion via a hot story. Tell her, and half Washington would know before he reached the Commuter's Rest Mortuary Chapel again.

As he pondered alone in his littered room, his eye struck the boxes of notes for his book. All at once the project seemed trivial.

What if—just *supposing*—he uncovered some sensational facts over there in Connecticut? Some monstrous conspiracy? He assumed he was the only one who knew anything about the underground organization, whatever its purpose. Certainly he was the only reporter. Opportunity beckoned. So did faint greed, he admitted.

Greed was unfamiliar to him—but probably only because of lack of opportunities. Hell, what harm would it do to write the exposé himself, if there was one to be written? Why shouldn't he get the credit for doing all the work and taking all the risks?

First, though, he must protect himself.

Next morning, instead of taking the usual vitamin break, he said to Joy, "I have to go out for a few minutes."

Joy folded up the edition of the paper she'd been studying. The front page carried a simulphoto of two cabinet members, the Secretary of Social Security and the Secretary of Fringe Benefits, cutting ribbons to open the new Birth Defects Insurance Administration Center.

"What're you after, love?" Joy asked. "Another dusty book that mentions your favorite colonel in small type in the appendix?"

"I need a new diary."

"Oh, that. You're a great one."

"Why do you say that?"

She pinched his arm, oblivious to the others in the newspaper mess. "I prefer my reflections printed in public, sweets, with my name above them, ten point or better. Cash in the bank is what I'm after."

Cassius grinned. "How do you know my diary won't make me famous one day?"

"That's what all diary-writers think. How many make it?"

Admitting she was right, and promising to meet her for lunch, Cassius left. He hurried down to an arcade on the fourth sub-level of the newspaper building. He bought an expensive diary at a stationery shop. The diary in which he'd been writing lately wasn't filled. But it was just a plain lockless diary. The one he purchased had a sonic lock: the first nine notes of the old folk song *Mister Clean,* whistled. The lock was tamperproof.

That night, after dinner with Joy, he went home and wrote down the events at the Ossining burial ground, as well as the location of the headquarters of the ring. Then he locked the new diary and went to bed, and dreamed the dog dream vividly.

The next night he set out for Connecticut.

He was unarmed. He was rather frightened. But he went.

He parked the Aircoupe down the block and walked. The moon was full. A gusty wind blew. Even here in the stews, where one tumbledown split-level housed a dozen squealing, fighting families, there was a sense and tang of earth's annual renewal. The wind carried the sweet breath of life. Turning up the mortuary walk, Cassius was suddenly conscious that he was approaching the age when men had instantly mortal coronaries.

He stopped on the walk, his uplifted face moonbathed, almost sad. The black dog seemed somewhere near.

He knocked quietly. He'd decided he wasn't the type to wave a gun or kick at locks. But his jaw fell when the door opened promptly.

Under a weak light stood a tall, rather soft man with receding hair, rimless glasses and brilliant blue eyes. The man wore grimy clothing. He looked slightly familiar.

"See here, my name is Cassius Andrews—"

"Of course," the man cut in. He smiled understandingly. "There's no need to take that tone. I've almost expected you to show up one day."

He held out his hand. "Come in, come in! Incidentally, my name is Kagle. Dr. Frederic."

VII

Before budging from the stoop, Cassius had to still his suspicions. "I mean to say, Kagle, what I came about is my brother. I want to know what happened to his body."

"Of course," the other repeated, as if it were only natural. "I'll be glad to tell you everything, Andrews. Not here on the doorstep, though. Come in and—oh." Frederic Kagle's eyes were intense and unwavering as blue gas flames. They took in Cassius's nervous glance at the dingy shadows in the hall. Dr. Kagle's manner became wry. "I see now. You expected something else. You still do. The latter-day Mafia or its equivalent. This is a perfectly legitimate research establishment."

And he reached around Cassius to grasp the door with a left hand whose ring finger bore the faint red ghost of a removed wedding band. He kept talking.

"We're a little under cover, I must admit. But we have our problems. I think you'll appreciate them once I explain. That is, if you've got the stomach to hear it all." A challenging glance. "Being a newsman, dedicated to truth in principle if not always in practice—I'm only speaking generically, of course—you should have an open mind if anyone does."

A small, confident smile played on Kagle's mouth. Cassius noted, however, that he secured the night chain on the door.

"I have to take your word that this operation is legitimate," Cassius said defensively. Kagle spun, peering hard. Cassius felt uncomfortable, as though he'd been tested and found wanting.

"Legitimate by my lights, is what I meant," Kagle said. "Some—my ex-wife among others—don't agree. I'll leave it up to your sense of fairness."

Cassius was fully aware of what Kagle was doing: using soft soap. But he was disarmed, temporarily anyway. Kagle led the way down the corridor which plainly hadn't been greatly renovated since the days when the place served as the final rest of thrombosis-stricken executives. Through two different doors jumbles of laboratory equipment winked faintly in the dark.

A third door was open, lighted. Kagle closed it quickly. He frowned, as over a minor annoyance. But not before Cassius had glimpsed more glass and metalware, and two men in spotted white coats.

One had been bending over sympathetically. The other had been seated on a stool, head on his forearms on a lucite bench, crying.

"Our work does have its personal problems too," Kagle said. He rolled back scrolled oak double doors. "Even dedicated people get shaky over the moral aspects now and then." He stood aside, waiting for Cassius to pass. Cassius caught the renewed flicker of blue intensity in the man's eye. The calm fire said that Kagle, a dedicated man, was not to be lumped with those who wallowed in shakiness.

Kagle rolled the doors shut again behind them.

The room was large, full of cheap, sharp-angled metal office furniture. A solar tube had been jerry-rigged in the wall. It shed a white, uncompromising light over all. The only signs of the room's former function were thick, threadbare carpeting, rose-petal wallpaper peeled in many places and an ancient framed motto, *I Am the Light of the World,* under which someone had taped a photo of some sort of molecular model.

Kagle circled the desk. He sat down, indicated Cassius's place.

"I think I'd better stand," Cassius said. "I didn't come here to be social."

"My dear Mr. Andrews," Kagle said gently, "you have every right to feel as you do. We should never have selected your brother. It was a mistake."

"Yes, it was. For you."

The scientist ignored the feigned toughness. "Ordinarily we try to choose people with no survivors. Last year, however, I had a fellow working for me." The blue-flame eyes brightened merrily. "My, shall we say, traffic manager? He proved to be an idiot. But he was all I could get. Now I handle that end myself. And have, ever since he slipped up a couple of times. One of his worst slip-ups was your brother the Reverend. It meant thirty hours' worth of work in a day instead of my usual twenty-six. But that's all right."

Cassius didn't do Kagle the favor of smiling even a little. "I want to know what you did with him."

Kagle didn't seem worried, just more amused. "So you can report us to the authorities?"

"Maybe. Well?"

Kagle pursed his lips. "Mr. Andrews, are you really tough enough to stand the truth?"

"I'm a newspaperman. I guess that qualifies me a little."

"Provided I tell you everything about your brother— which will mean in turn telling you everything about what we do here, and why I'm reduced to crawling out at night like some roach just so I can conduct a perfectly legitimate scientific study—will you promise in return not to write one word about what I say?"

Abruptly Cassius sat down. He fought to keep a straight face. A moment ago he'd been cowed by the man's assured, almost jocular manner. Now it was his turn to feel like laughing.

If the man was indeed a scientist, he was the stereotype: foolish, naive, unworldly beneath his veneer of hard-lipped dedication. What a hell of a stupid offer! Did Kagle honestly think he would pass up a chance for an exposé now that he had the material practically in his hands? He had to write what he learned. For Timothy's sake.

And for his own, too. He'd seen a glimmer of a real chance to improve his lot. Such a chance hadn't come his way in longer than he could remember. He'd almost believed he was no longer interested in opportunities. Sitting across from Kagle, he discovered otherwise.

Carefully, softly, he lied, "All right, Dr. Kagle. If that's your price, I promise."

The sap fell for it at once. "Thank you."

Why were the blue eyes merry a moment? Or was it a trick of the light? Kagle tented his fingers, leaned across the desk.

"First tell me how you found me."

"No harm in that, I guess." Cassius described his speculations, starting with those initiated the night he heard Madame Wanda Kagle ranting. "I'll admit I didn't dream she really had any connection with you. Or with Timothy. It was just sort of a—well, trigger."

Kagle shook his head. "Poor sis. She badgered me until I showed her."

A trickle of sweat, unbidden, rolled down Cassius's cheek. "Showed her what?"

"The results of our research here into the nature of death."

"The nature of—?" Cassius's eyes bugged.

Dr. Kagle leaned back, chuckling. His pink forehead shone. "There it is again. You imagine we're a bunch of necrophiles, don't you? Nothing so debased, Mr. Andrews, though in certain quarters we're certainly regarded in that light. What we're doing is simply probing the experience of dying from a qualitative standpoint. I could give you a long lecture on the theory. But in plainest terms, our work is this. I'm a neurosurgeon by training. What I do with all the dead bodies I'm forced to steal is analogous to what a man in a darkroom does when he develops film. He brings forth the latent image. A photo's latent image is both there and not there, in the silver. It awaits the right combination of chemicals before it becomes visible. So with the—" Dr. Kagle hesitated a second, as if gauging Cassius's nerve again. "—call it the latent image of death. Or images. The sensory record of the last microseconds before the mind blacks out. All the pain. All the smells, tactile sensations. The blurred sights. When I was killing time as just another white-coated bureaucrat with the Institutes of Health, I worked out techniques which would parallel the first formulation of the proper photochemicals. And that's why I need the bodies, Mr. Andrews. What good is a darkroom technician without exposed film?"

Kagle paused. "Do you want me to go into the surgical and electronic techniques more deeply?"

"No. Let me get this straight." Cassius was sweating hard. "You're able to take someone's—corpse—and from it get a record of what it felt like for that person to die?"

"That is more or less it, yes. The process involves a great deal of painstaking surgery, much work with computers and video tape and sound-recording equipment. I tried to get the Institutes to underwrite the initial study. Naturally they wouldn't, they didn't dare. You're too young—and so am I, though perhaps I don't look it—to remember the DNA Riots when Gadsburry finally created one single cell in his lab. I'm sure you've read about the riots often. Old illusions die hard, Mr. Andrews. Some of mine died, too, when I first took up this field. I wanted to work legally. Obtain legitimate corpses in the manner of a private medical school."

"Couldn't you?"

The blue-flame eyes brightened. "A court order obtained by a committee of certain members of the clergy in this country frustrated my efforts. I decided it was prudent to go underground, so to speak. To steal the bodies I needed. After all, I'm convinced in my own mind that the work is necessary, important. And honest. Men have been martyred before. I'm prepared to be martyred myself, though of course I prefer to avoid it."

More amusement suddenly. "And I've discovered it won't be necessary, either, Mr. Andrews."

"Isn't this very expensive research?"

"Frightfully."

"Then where—?"

Kagle shrugged. "Patents. Three big ones, several small ones. Neurosurgical apparatus. The royalties are more than ample."

Cassius said, "But I don't really understand why you chose to work in this particular field."

Kagle sounded sad. "After I stumbled across the fundamental technique, it wasn't a matter of choosing."

"Your reason is—?"

"To know. What else?"

"I can see why the clergy would stand in your way."

"Frankly," Kagle snapped, "I can't. I'm not in any way tampering with their precious concepts of immortality. Of course I am in a position to state that, as far as sentient experience goes, there is no immortality after the act of death. The neural latent images are feeble at best by the time I'm through scrounging for the bodies. And they quickly go altogether. Yet even though I resent the opposition, I've tried to be circumspect. Picked subjects who fit my requirements—a violent death, for maximum image strength—but have no relatives or family. I've done this partly out of vestigial moral considerations, partly from a practical wish to avert discovery and continue my studies as long as possible. With your brother, as I stated, the fool I had working for me slipped up. You were shrewd enough to locate me. Therefore I'll hide nothing, Mr. Andrews. I'm no criminal."

Cassius frowned. "Are you sure? What you're doing touches on realms other than the purely scientific."

Kagle sighed. "Metaphysics? I'm only concerned about that as it relates to the people—the clerics—who prate about it and therefore act because of it. I don't want to be dragged into a lot of messy court trials. Which is exactly what would happen if this work became public. Trials, more trials, publicity and, eventually, other harmful effects, evidences of which you saw in my sister's behavior. I'm really going to have to do something about her soon."

Cassius felt as if he should draw back, flee. But he was oddly unable.

"About my brother's body. Where is it?"

"Ruined, I'm afraid. Gone. The techniques we use are destructive. That's why there mustn't be relatives."

"What happens to your so-called latent images?"

"We record them. Five separate tracks which can be projected simultaneously for a viewer. Though viewing is a dull, limited term for the experience."

"So a person—knows how it feels to die?"

"Yes. By violence. The most painful deaths possible. Raises some interesting speculations, doesn't it? I think you intimated that Wanda was mouthing some of them. Quite apart from the empiric achievement of translating and recording a dying body's sensory images, the research opened up whole new areas of less tangible results. I only began to think about some of the related questions after the work was well under way. Namely, do people fear the *what* of death, or do they fear the *how* and its lesser partner, the *when?*"

"For myself," Cassius said slowly, "I—I'm afraid of the end. The blankness. The finality."

"Are you? I assure you there is evidence to the contrary. Death must be a little like sleep. Before you sleep, what is going to happen while you sleep is rationally graspable. The sleep of death is permanent. So you can't reconcile yourself to it wholly. But you can begin to reconcile yourself to it, if only slightly. While I don't think you can reconcile yourself to the other part reasonably. To the pain. The anguish. The lifetime of hells in one instant, one instant waiting, always waiting up there ahead. It's my contention that, because of innumerable variables not present in the sleep aspect, the pain of death can only be known when it happens. And the variables only increase the terror."

"The theory won't hold up," Cassius said. "Death, the absolute end—that's the fearful part."

"Ah, you assume that because everybody's always assumed it. I assumed so too. All I can say is, my work has revealed evidence to the contrary. Evidence no open-minded person can deny. Which is why I made you promise not to write a word."

Abruptly Cassius felt the thrust of ambition, possibilities, chances like gold. He tried to fix the lines of his face and sound demanding:

"Look, Kagle. So far all you've given me is a lot of talk. If you've recorded these so-called latent images, then they ought to be available for someone to see, right?"

"See is another poor word. Experience would be more correct."

"All right, experience, see, view, you name it. But I want it demonstrated."

"You have more courage than I thought."

"Listen, Kagle, you can't scare me. What about it?"

"If you'll hold to your promise not to write—"

"I will, yes," Cassius lied, feeling very foxy and, incidentally, very righteous.

Weren't those gas-jet eyes laughing at him all at once again?

He was puzzled. Kagle was a naive fool. Maybe Cassius only saw laughter in the eyes. The man wasn't mad, Cassius was positive of that much. Yet his confidence ebbed quickly. He had the feeling he oughtn't to go through with what he himself had suggested.

But the copy possibilities—! My God! Staggering.

"Since you volunteer, Mr. Andrews, let's step down the hall." Dr. Kagle rose, smoothing his thin hair. "I'll show you as little or as much as you find you're able to stand. This way, please."

VIII

The chamber at the rear of the funeral home had been renovated with theater seats to resemble a private projection room minus the screen. Cassius took a place in the front row center. Dr. Kagle wheeled over a cart on which were mounted several odd-looking instruments. From the instruments dangled fifteen or twenty wires which ended in assorted pads and needles.

"It'll take me a few minutes to get you wired up properly," Dr. Kagle said, snapping a leather cuff around Cassius's bare left forearm. There was unmistakable pride in his eyes as he worked. "I apologize in advance for the needle pricks, but they're necessary."

Cassius was sweating harder. He was fearful but determined to go through with it. He pointed beyond his boot.

"What's that for?"

"The pedal?" It was corrugated iron, painted red. "Just put your left foot on it. There, perfect. If at any point you want to stop, press down. All five tracks will come to a halt simultaneously. Which people do you want?"

"I don't care. Butcher—" Cassius gasped as a needle went home in his thigh. "Butcher Balk? He was the one really responsible for my being here. And Timothy, if that's possible."

"Certainly. I'll also show you one or two others for the sake of contrast. Are you quite sure you're up to it, though?"

"Hell yes," Cassius said, with more conviction than he felt.

"Very well." Dr. Kagle kept working, presently stood back. "Got you trussed up, eh? Any of the pads chafe too much? Good. I'll be leaving. The console is in the next room. There's no need to close your eyes. The lights will dim. Then you won't see a thing in here. You'll be—But explanations are inadequate. Remember the pedal, Mr. Andrews. I won't be offended if you use it."

A door chunked shut. Cassius peered through the crisscross of wires padded to his temples. He blinked. His vision was failing.

No, it was only the dimming of solar sheets across the ceiling. Dimming fast, from pearl to ebony to nothing. Must adjust the boot on the pedal, he thought, in case it's so harrowing I—

Blur-and-whine.

A light bulb way up there. Weak, shaded with a scrap of tin.

He shifted his head. The rusted springs of the rickety cot squeaked. Suthin needs fixin with the furnace. About this time at night I got to fix the furnace but I can't remember what it is needs fixing. Suthin's wrong.

A slow, labored turn of his head. Difficulty seeing because a film of water was on the eyes. Blinking didn't help. A monster old metal furnace hulked in a corner of the musty storeroom. He could barely read the nameplate. EUREKA! *E-Z Draught No. 22.* EUREKA COMFORT WORKS, *Eureka, Iowa.*

In his chest he felt the annoying, clotted little pain.

Ah Momma I can see your face right now. I been havin trouble sleepin lately Momma. Little pains in the middle. I can see you Momma, I can hear you singin and playin the piano Momma like you did on Sundays.

In his throat the breath caught. He lifted himself, blinked the eye-water back. He saw a faded, patched quilt over his chest, hands on top of it, shaking. They were ancient, wrinkled hands with thickened blue veins standing out.

The Doc don't make me work so hard these days because of the pains but the furnace needs fixin and I wonder what's wrong with m—Momma my God I'm dyin that's what's wrong.

He remembered forgotten music, *The Old Rugged Cross,* with the bass hand beaten out in Sunday-morning rhythm, *thrummm, thrummm, thrummm.*

Fearful, he tried to cry aloud for help. He couldn't make a sound. The clotting pain, a small hurting ball inside him, widened. It troubled and troubled him. Not the pain itself, which wasn't so bad. Knowing what the pain meant.

Momma I'm goin to be seein you. I don't want it to happen like this I—

The Eureka furnace sank into darkness and sucked all the light after it.

Blur-and-whine.

"Brucie? Brucie? Oh God Brucie, don't!" his wife was screaming.

Against his palms, under his boots, the pebbled poly of the hotel wall and ledge. On his lips a queer saltiness, blood he'd drawn biting down, getting up the guts to do it.

The wind was blowing hard. It whistled and smelled of the pollution of Lake Erie. Ten stories below a crowd had collected in the Public Square. For miles he could see the lights of Cleveland, warm whites and yellows.

They were snares and delusions. The lights were behind doors of understanding, friendship, love, shut to him, shut to him every one—

"Officer, officer!" his wife screamed. "Don't let Brucie do it! Go out and get him. The poor children—"

He jumped.

The wind tugged at his palms, his cheeks. The lights blurred. His bowels loosened. Vertical rows of lights blurred and became a single strip as he hurtled down. Wind hammered his eardrums. He was falling fast, faster—

The hit was explosion. Body's total scream. Coalescing of sensation into one enormous burst of pain—

PAIN PAIN PAIN PAIN PAIN PA—

Blur-and-whine.

Behind the effin glass in the visitor's gallery the effin newsmen were already talkin on their effin portable visors.

He ran his tongue over his rough, dry lips. His scalp felt prickly where they'd wiped it bare with that effin aerosol. Under his strapped arms the porcelain chair was cold.

Somewhere behind, footsteps, as the last effin attendant shuffled out. A door closed.

The room had a funny smell. It was prolly cause of the green walls, so effin clean an sanitary like a hospital, like a place for killin bugs. Well he wasn't no bug.

He bunched his face muscles to show he had guts. One of the effin newsmen, a fairy with ringlets, was watchin him and talkin in the visor. He was sure he saw the effer's mouth make the words, "Butcher Balk is now sitting in the chair ladies and gentlemen."

All at once, without wanting to, he was pulling against the cuffs and leg straps. They hurt. "Oh no, oh no, please Jesus, I—"

Something whacked softly like a toggle jamming between contacts. Lights dimmed. Eyes?

Pain was beginning. A stiff, ghastly tickling that instantly doubled, tripled, quadrupled, multiplying, multiplying, a rising blast of dreadful murdering pain—

PAIN PAIN PAIN PAIN PA—

Blur-and-whine.

"—outa this! You stay out or ge' killed," de Diego chanted. "You watch it, Christer, I'm warnin' you."

Tipsy, back and forth, faces in the cheap bar swung. His hands were ineffectual, soft, untrained for struggle. He tried to hold both the right shoulder of de Diego, the left shoulder of Ratface Lats. The three of them struggled, roiling the amphet vapors thick in the bar.

"Watch out Revrun Tim," one of the whores cried. "He gotta knife."

"I tell you you must not take each other's life," he shouted, fighting between them, vocal cords nearly raw.

Something jerked at his left shoulder. Spun him fast. De Diego's drug-swollen eyes loomed. Silver flashed in his hand.

"I warn you din I Christer?" was the scream, and suddenly a hole was in him, and tears tasting on his lips.

The hole widened in his stomach. He could feel de Diego actually wrenching and driving the knife into him, down into his bowels to the bottom, bringing in one unforeseen torrent a dimming of his eyes, and no time even to think a prayer as he tottered, everything blurred beneath pain—

PAIN PAIN PAIN PA—

Crash, crash, like a madman Cassius hammered his

boot on the pedal, where was it, it must be there, *crash, crash.*

Drool was on his lips. His head was thrown back, wrenching, the eyes shut. Wires snapped as he wrenched, his leg going up and down like a mad thing, *crash, crash, crash—*

"Stop it! Stop it! Stop it! Stop it! Stop it!"

IX

Limp, drained, Cassius leaned one arm on the ledge of the Aircoupe blister. His left leg hadn't yet stopped trembling.

The moon sailed high and round over the Westport slums. A shadow disengaged from the night, leaned close to the little car. For a moment Cassius had trouble recognizing or remembering.

Then everything washed back. His hands clawed on the blister ledge. He strained up, thrashing at impossible terror all around.

"There, there, take it easy," said Kagle. The grip on his arm steadied him. Cassius sank back down in the bucket seat.

"How did I get out here?"

"I carried you after I unstrapped you. You fainted. I'm sorry about that last sequence. But you did specifically ask for it. I have a bottle of brandy in my office. It might help. Do you want to go back inside?"

Cassius buried his face in his hands. "Christ, no. Christ."

After several seconds he raised his head again. At last he was gaining control. "Kagle, you're a goddamn monster, that's what you are. What you have in there—it—it's—" He shivered. No one word could encompass it.

Cynical tolerance tinged Kagle's lips in the moonlight. "No, Andrews. You're wrong. It's only the truth. Death as it really is."

Cassius swiped at his moist upper lip. "Who was that first one? That smelly old man?"

Dr. Kagle looked quite interested. "Why do you ask?"

"Because—it wasn't as bad as the rest."

"Interesting. I found that to be the case myself. That was old Peckham. He used to be the janitor here. I kept him on to do odd jobs. He was eighty-six and nearly senile when he died in the middle of the night one night, of simple old age."

"That was—just an ordinary death?"

"Yes. Did you find it painful?"

"A little. Not as bad as—the others. Not nearly as bad."

Dr. Kagle went, "Um. After I'd begun my work, it occurred to me to look into at least one natural, quiet death by way of contrast. Peckham's latent images were quite weak. But they surprised me. I've done a couple of similar analyses since. The so-called quiet, ordinary death has a minimum of pain associated with it, but it's all quite bearable. So you see, Mr. Andrews, I think that what we really fear is the awful pain of a violent end." Kagle paused. He peered down sharply. "Or don't you grasp the significance?"

Hardly hearing, Cassius blurted, "I'll write about this. Expose this dirty business."

"Mr. Andrews, I don't think you will."

"There's something indecent about—what did you say? Oh. My promise. Well, I lied to you."

"I know you did."

Cassius stared.

"But that's all right, Andrews. I let you lie to make it seem you were putting something over on me. That you were fooling me into permitting you to see the tracks. When Flange and his toughs came here right after the court order business, he also threatened me, Mr. Andrews. Arrest. A treason trial. You name it. I appeared to be frightened, pliant. I explained my work. I told him I'd let him judge for himself, and if he thought I was a criminal, I would submit to arrest. I let him sit in the same chair you occupied. And then his men, one at a time. Flange hasn't bothered me since. That's why I let you see, Andrews. In a way, you and Flange and Wanda are part of the surprising evidence that's begun to come in. Evidence that it isn't the long sleep we fear after all but the how that's our lash and spur. The unknown, potentially horrible *how*. There is some reason to fear it if we die in bed, but monumental reason if our death turns out to be violent. As you saw."

Cassius's mind was still slow. It grabbed at phrases: "Flange? He came here? You bastard."

Kagle nodded. "Yes. I must say he and his men bore up rather well. So did my sister Wanda. They all endured the tracks to the end."

"Trying to say I'm a coward?" Cassius choked. "Trying to say—"

"Don't be belligerent," Kagle cut in gently. "The only reason you reacted so violently back inside was because of the intensely personal connection. Your brother was dying, not some stranger. The human body, mind, are surprisingly resilient. The endurance is remarkable." Kagle seemed sad. "Yet isn't it strange how men and women don't know their own strength? Think they must protect themselves? Make themselves safe, secure?"

Cassius glowered. "Quit it, Kagle. Weepy expressions don't fool me. You don't give a God damn for anybody else."

Kagle seemed to muse over this. "In a sense perhaps that's true. Else I wouldn't be in this peculiar work. Or intending to go ahead with it, as I am. But I am rather sorry for you, Mr. Andrews."

The "Hah!" from Cassius was short, cackling, grotesque.

"Oh, I realize you don't believe me, but I truly am sorry in my own way. I shouldn't have put you through it. I should have been aware of the personal element. Also, I should have avoided it because I'm beginning to see the pattern which I hinted about. In the aftereffects, I mean."

Suddenly Kagle leaned close to the Aircoupe again. For the first time there was raw, fundamental emotion on his face:

"If it became widely known that I could arrange such experiences I'd have no peace. No, I can't let you write, Mr. Andrews. For if they came after me *en masse*, there'd be no end. Don't you see what I could offer them? That is to say—" Eyes haunted now. "—if I would, which I won't, because I know where it would lead?"

"No," Cassius said, low. "I don't see."

"I could say to them, come to me, steel yourself, prepare to endure five minutes of the most agonizing pain on this earth. Live through the most anguished of deaths, the most violent. Then you'll be free the rest of your life. Free because the worst will be over. Free because, statistically, don't you see, you and millions like you won't ever die so violently. You'll die the lesser death of a Peckham, with only a bit of eminently endurable pain. Nothing near the kind of pain which, say, that criminal endured."

Cassius snickered. "Who'd fall for that?"

"Many, Mr. Andrews. In fact I believe most. I won't pretend it's a riskless proposition, I'd have to say to them. You might, just might, be one of the few in ten millions who will die violently one day. But the risk is infinitesimal. While the reward—well, I could say, if you go through the ultimate, the worst now, think of the years ahead. The years of not having to fear, always fear the unknowable. Dying a Peckham's death then would be child's play, don't you see? And should you lose the gamble—die a violent death after all, I would say—why, then even it might be a whit less terrible. Of course the real benefit, I would say, lies in the years free of fear. If that sounds like a foolish offer, Mr. Andrews, five minutes of hell in exchange for a lifetime of release from the terror dying holds—if it sounds illogical that anyone would accept—if you believe people wouldn't clamor for it—then I submit, Andrews, that you don't know a damn thing about the nature of the world you're living in."

"No one would want—" Cassius began, unsure.

"Wouldn't they? Are you aware of the temper of men's minds over the past eighty years? What do most people desire of life anymore, Mr. Andrews? To be secure against the harms of life. Don't ask me why. Perhaps we'll never understand all the complicated reasons lost back in the years. But people want it. The price keeps rising, but they still want it. I could give it to them. At the price of being Butcher Balk for five short minutes. And they can stand it. Wanda stood it. Flange stood it. Afterward, there'd be *nothing left to fear*. The world is peopled with Peckhams, not Butcher Balks, Mr. Andrews."

Then, slowly, Kagle sighed. "But I'll never say any of that, Mr. Andrews. I'll never say I could pull fear's fangs, simply because I know they'd want it. They wouldn't be satisfied with less than everything once they heard. Not until they learned the real price. Not until it was too late. Not until the world's engine stopped."

"Yours hasn't stopped," Cassius snarled.

"No," Kagle said, almost sad again. "But then I've never permitted myself to experience more than two senses of any subject at any one time."

His pale hand lifted, in the general direction of the moon high above the world, as if to say the subject was at last exhausted. Flickering on his face were the expressions of two men, one the god, one the assassin of everything.

The god could have slain the assassin by surrendering his godhood in suicide. Being a god, he couldn't quite. No, said the gas-blue eyes, he couldn't quite, ever.

"Good night, Mr. Andrews." Dr. Kagle definitely sounded weary. "I know it's been too harrowing. But you did ask me about your brother. What choice did I have?"

Muttering all the obscenities he knew, Cassius jammed

his card into the ignition slot and rammed the Aircoupe away from the vicinity of the funeral parlor, leaving the blister open so he could shout back, "You rotten bastard, I'll tell the world about this, I'll let them know—"

X

The Etaoin Pub was located on the fourth sub-level of the Capitol World Truth Building.

The pneumodoor went *hush-hush* open, then closed. Cassius heard it dimly. He was slumped over the bar, looking at his globe of Old Kentuckye Woodesman 120 Proof Sippin' Sauce.

He heard footsteps. He continued to peer into the amber infinity of the booze. Who the hell cared about footsteps?

"Cassius? It is you! Good God in heaven, sweets, what's happened?"

The barkeep ambled over. "Friend of yours, lady?"

"You're new around here."

"Yeah. Hired on two weeks ago."

"This man works on the paper upstairs."

The barkeep sniggered. "When?"

"What?"

"Lady, this guy's been campin' here since the day I started."

Fuzzily Cassius recognized the voice of Joy de Veever. His body felt weighted with bags of lead shot. It was an effort merely to turn and blink his red eyes slowly, like an owl.

Joy had something clasped in her arms. Her glance was alternately indignant and sympathetic.

"I should have thought of coming to this bar sooner, Cassius. But you're not the drinking type."

"Every time some of the boys from the paper come in," said the barkeep, "he goes to the john. First time, when he didn't come out for a while, I thought he was sick. Went back there myself. He was just standing. Told me to leave him alone. I did. When the boys left after lunch, he came out. Same routine in the evening, too. Sometimes he leaves but he always comes back. Wonder where he goes at ni—"

"Thanks for your help," Joy cut in. "I'll take over. Cassius?"

"Lee me lone," he said, finding it like climbing Everest to gesture.

"Cassius, what in God's name is the trouble?"

Getting no answer, Joy pulled up the next stool. She told the barkeep she wanted nothing to drink. The tone clearly instructed him to leave. He did. Cassius blinked at the object in Joy's hand. Some sort of book with a tricky shining clasp.

"Cassius love, I've been searching for you ever since I got back yesterday. It's apparent that I shouldn't have spent that week and a half in Bonn at the Floorwax Institute trade show." She sounded affronted. "In the interval it seems you've completely lost your mind."

"Perfly all right." His tongue was oh so heavy. "Perfly."

"Perfectly my eye! I just talked to Hughgenine upstairs."

"Bothrin me. Come in here and bother me. I didn't make it to the men's in time."

"Bothering! I should hope so! After all, when you don't show up to work for sixteen days straight, it's natural for him to bother. Cassius—darling—" And the tears were genuine all at once, rolling down over her rouged cheeks. "Are you in trouble? Hughgenine said he lost his temper. He's sorry he fired you on the spot. He'll take you back if only you'll tell somebody what's wrong. Cassius? Wake up and listen to me! You're being horrid. You don't know the agony I've been through. Last night I nearly had your floor super thinking you'd suffered a heart attack and must be lying dead inside your flat. What hit that place? Your books were all torn apart."

"So wat?" he inquired. "So wat, so wat? Joy lee me lone."

"I will not leave you alone! I'll get you to a doctor. Do something! Are you having a nervous breakdown, sweetheart? To destroy your things that way—all the notes for the biography of that colonel strewn all over in pieces—"

"Stupid book. Useless goddam wase time."

"Are you in trouble with some woman, Cassius?"

He giggled, but it had a dull sound.

"Cassius, I must say it again. You're treating me very unkindly. After all, you do mean something to me, you know. Please, please, please tell me what's wrong."

"Oh nothin. I just got a tase for booze, 's all."

"Obviously." Joy couldn't help sounding smug. "And obviously you're in no shape to help anybody who wishes to help you, whether it's Hughgenine or me or anyone. That's why I brought this. I figured if the answer can't be gotten from you, it can be gotten from this. Unless you've lost your mind so thoroughly you've broken every single habit you ever had."

She was extending the object in her hand. The clasp looked vaguely familiar. Why did he feel alarmed?

"I found your other diary too, Cassius. In pieces. This one was intact."

"Too tough," he muttered. "Too dam tough tear up. Hey." Again he blinked. "Snoopin?"

"Yes, snooping. I admit it. I had to find some explanation for the peculiar, awful way you're behaving. Now you tell me how to open this lock, Cassius. Either that or you tell me what's the matter with you. Else I'll go to the stationer's where you bought it. See, the name's stamped in gold on the back. It's right on this level. I'll force them to disclose the code."

"Gimme tha," he said, lifting his eighty-pound hand, trying to thrust it through the gloomy darkness of the bar.

The effort cracked away some of his lethargy. He felt he must have the diary in his possession. Then he knew why. The last entry mentioned the Commuter's Rest Mortuary Chapel by name. Didn't it?

He wasn't positive. He thought so. Warning bells, so faint he barely heard them.

"I will not." Joy held the book miles away. "I will not give it to you."

"I said gimme—!" he cried, standing. He toppled on his face.

From afar, Joy said to the barkeep, "You watch him. This man's sick. I'm going to get this book opened and then we'll take him to a hospital. You just watch him a few minutes. No, you shut up, do as I say! Want to lose your job? The paper owns this building, leases this space, or aren't you aware of that? Here, Cassius. Stand up."

As he fumbled his way back to the stool with her help, he managed to perceive what it meant. Joy, poor old Joy. Sure she wanted to help. Sure. The locked diary tantalized her. Anything that might harbor a scrap of something hot tantalized her.

Paper leased the space? For the stationer's too, probably. They'd come across with the code under threat. He made one more abortive lunge for the book.

He grabbed the poly bar rim to keep from falling. He could see it now. He didn't actually care but he felt he should. The book would open to a tune whose notes and name he couldn't recall. Then Joy's curious eyes. They'd glitter, running down the entries.

Then showing it to Hughgenine. Then the trail to Kagle. Joy's hot one, the big hot one in reach at last. Plus her sense of avenging him. As if that mattered.

Christ. What Kagle had said was true, true. First one person would have—he shuddered and knuckled his eyes and moaned a little—those experiences. Then the next would have to see what the experience was. Then the next after that. Then someone would see how it could pull the fangs of fear. Go through the worst, the very worst, and your imagination won't have anything to gnaw on, year after year. Wanda Kagle put it right. *I've been there.*

Christ, the government and the do-gooders would probably seize everything. The public good. Uplift. You can stand five minutes of Butcher Balk to be free, can't you? Take a chance, you're bound to die like Peckham. Think of the peace. *I've been there.*

Dimly he recalled the thousands on the waiting lists of the Securo Corporation. They'd want it. Everyone would want it but a few who, like Kagle, might see the threat. They would cry out. Their cries would be lost in the howls of happiness. *Get it over. Nothing so bad ever again.*

I've been there.

Did they know what it would do? Did they care? No, they wouldn't care, they'd weep for joy as it multiplied, on, on, to the ends of the earth—

But though he knew these things in a dim way, he couldn't put them all into words. It took too much effort.

"Worl's engine," Cassius whimpered. "Joy don, worl's engine."

Or had he said it aloud at all? He wasn't sure. He'd made the effort in his skull. Whether the effort had stirred his voice box, lips, tongue, he couldn't say. He felt so immeasurably tired. He crawled back up on the stool. Even his sense of urgency, alarm, had aborted. No longer could he be sure why he'd spoken. It certainly couldn't have been for any good reason. He didn't have any good reasons.

Still, something made him squeak it once more, "Worl's engine."

The barkeep clucked his tongue. "Mister? The lady can't hear you."

A feeble whisper, dying: "Worl's engine."

"Mister, you're dreaming. The lady left."

That roused him a little. "Use have a dream. This dog. Chasin me. Not anymore. No dreams since—"

The sentence dribbled off. It didn't seem worth finishing. Only the drink. His hand crawled out. Only the drink seemed worth finishing. And he wasn't even certain about that, really.